The Urbana Free Library

To renew: call 217-367-4057
or go to *"urbanafreelibrary.org"*
and select "Renew/Request Items"

THIRST

Forthcoming by Andrei Gelasimov:

The Lying Year
Rachel
The Gods of the Steppe

7-12

THIRST

ANDREI GELASIMOV
Translated by Marian Schwartz

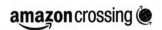

7/12
149

Thirst by Andrei Gelasimov was first published in 2003 by Eksmo
Publishers in Moscow as Zhazhda.

Translated from the Russian by Marian Schwartz.
First published in English in 2011 by AmazonCrossing.

Published by AmazonCrossing
P.O. Box 400818
Las Vegas, NV 89140

ISBN-13: 9781611090697
ISBN-10: 1611090695
Library of Congress Control Number: 2011907216

THIRST

All the vodka wouldn't fit in the fridge. First I tried standing the bottles up, and then I laid them on their sides, one on top of the other. The bottles stacked up like transparent fish. Then they hunkered down and stopped clinking. But ten or so just wouldn't fit.

I should have told my mother to take this refrigerator back a long time ago. It's an affront to me and the little boy next door. Every night this monster cuts in full blast, and he cries on the other side of the wall. And my vodka is never all going to go in. It's too damn small.

Fucking pig.

So I had to put it on the shelf. And the windowsill. And the floor. Same old same old. One I put in the bathroom, the dirty clothes hamper. I thought, Why the hell not? Just in case.

When I was done with the vodka more or less, someone started ringing at my door. At first I didn't want to open up because it was late, but then I did anyway. It had to be Olga. Not even my mother had stopped by in half a year. We communicated by phone.

"I'm sorry to bother you again," she said. "My Nikita's acting up. Please help me out this once. I can't cope with him by myself."

"No problem," I said.

I threw on a jacket and went out. I even left my door open.

"Well then, who here doesn't want to go to bed?"

The little guy shuddered and stared at me as if I were a ghost. He actually dropped his blocks.

"Who here isn't listening to his mama?"

He was looking at me, speechless. Only his eyes got as big as saucers.

"Come on, get your things," I said. "Since you don't want to listen to your mama, you're going to be living with me. You get to take one toy."

He was absolutely speechless, and his mouth was open very wide.

"Which one are we going to take? The car or this guy? Who is this you have here? Superman, is it? Come on, take your Superman along."

He shifted his eyes to Olga and whispered:

"I'll go to bed. Mama, I'll go to bed all by myself right away."

"What a smart boy. You catch on quick. If anything like this happens again, I'm going to come back and take you with me for real."

Olga stopped me by the door.

"Would you like some tea? We can go into the kitchen. I just brewed some up."

"I left my door open there. You never know..."

Then she said, "You have to forgive me for bothering you all the time. It's just that he...you're the only person he's afraid of. He's stopped listening to me completely."

I grunted.

"Makes sense. I would've been even more afraid if I were him. How old is he?"

"Five. Four years and ten months."

"I would've been even more afraid."

"Please forgive me...Just don't be insulted, please."

Then we didn't say anything for a while.

"It's perfectly all right. If anything comes up, be sure to stop by. I'm going to be staying home now. I finished a job. I got all my money."

She looked at me.

"Are you going to be drinking vodka for the next three months again?"

"Where'd you get that idea? I just sit home and watch TV."

She looked at me and smiled. Not very cheerfully, I must say.

"Fine, forgive me one more time. You too be sure to stop by if anything comes up. You really wouldn't like some tea?"

At home I walked over to the mirror and stood in front of it for a long time. I looked at what had become of me.

If only Seryoga hadn't been wrong back then and hadn't left me to burn up last in the APC. But he thought I was already done for. That's why he pulled the others out first. The ones who were still showing signs of life.

Which means I'm only good for frightening naughty kids now. Olga lucked out with me for a neighbor.

– – –

But when we first started construction trade school, they lined us all up in front of the building, and the head teacher said, "You are now the face of the construction industry. Don't let your fathers down." But who was there to let down, really? Our head teacher was obviously out of the loop. Instead of fathers at home we had our Uncle Ediks. In the singular, of course. But the head teacher meant all of us standing in front of him, even though it had started raining and the trees had lost nearly all their leaves. That's why he was speaking in the plural. While we stood there in front of him shivering with cold. No one had warned us that the lineup would take so long. So we had left our jackets in the workshops. And no one had taken cigarettes, naturally. But maybe he was right as far as the generalizations went. Who knows? Maybe by then each one of us had his own Uncle Edik sitting in the kitchen.

Mama would say, "Only you don't have to go making that face. Eduard Mikhailovich is helping us out. If it weren't for him, do you know where you and I might have wound up? Your father never even gave us the time of day. Not before the divorce for sure, and after it he just spat on us. Do you know where we might have wound up?"

But I didn't. And Eduard Mikhailovich wasn't Eduard Mikhailovich to me. And he sure as hell wasn't Uncle Edik. To me he was nobody. I didn't even say "him" if I wanted to tell my mother something. I just mumbled incoherently and jerked my head. But she understood. It's just every time she would say, "You don't have to go making that face."

But I remembered how she and my father and I used to go sunbathing in the summer, and he would always wear these white shorts, to show off his tan, because he tanned easily and handsomely. He wore this very classy cap and shimmery, multicolored glasses. He never sat with us on the blanket. He would circle around it or stand a little ways away or play volleyball. Or laugh with the tanned, young girls. While Mama and I would hide from the sun under our umbrella.

She would tell me, "Kostya, you got my skin. You can't tan with skin like that. Too many freckles. Come on, I'll rub some cream on you. Otherwise your whole face is going to burn up."

— — —

5

Olga opened the door almost immediately. She probably hadn't even had time to undress little Nikita.

"Did you change your mind about the tea? Good for you. Go on into the kitchen. I'll put Nikita to bed right now."

I waited for her in the hall, and when she came back from the nursery I said I didn't want any tea.

I just needed her to show me where to nail up the mirror I had for her. I mean, just set it down. Because it was late now and Nikita had gone to bed. So it didn't make any sense to hammer a nail into the wall now, naturally. Then there were the neighbors. Although, besides Olga and me there was just one old man on our landing. And he was deaf. But still, there was Nikita. So it would be better first thing tomorrow morning. For now I just needed to set the mirror down somewhere.

She looked at me in silence and then pointed toward the corner. Directly under the coatrack. There was already a mirror hanging on the other wall. The same kind of round mirror. But a little bigger than mine.

I straightened up.

"It was just leftover from my mother. They moved a long time ago, but they left a few things behind…That stupid refrigerator. It must keep your Nikita awake, I'll bet."

"No, it doesn't bother him."

Then I took a look at her vestibule and said it was time for some renovations. She smiled and replied that she couldn't afford it.

"How much would you charge?"

"I only do Euro renovations. For rich people. Double-glazed windows, dropped ceilings—all kinds of crud."

"Well, but still. How much?"

"Oh, eighty, a hundred thousand. Sometimes as much as a hundred and twenty."

"You're kidding!"

"They've got plenty of dough. They have to rub each other's noses in it."

She smiled.

"They've got a hard life."

I smiled, too.

"Yeah, real tough."

– – –

Because I really didn't know who had stiffed whom. Whether Genka had stiffed Pashka or vice versa. Although each of them accused the other of chicanery, naturally. They took turns coming to see me in their SUVs and saying, Oh, you know I couldn't stiff him. Go on, say it. You know it's true.

And I said I knew because I couldn't tell them no. Either one. I didn't actually know the truth. Not that I wanted to. Who gave a damn about that? When you burn up in an APC with someone—after that a lot of things start looking very different. They were just lucky. Seryoga pulled them out a little sooner. First them; then this weird captain from division headquarters; after him the driver, Mikhalich; then Ensign Demidov; and after everyone else, finally, me.

Maybe it was because they were lucky that they later decided to stiff each other. I don't know. Money's a terrible thing. I wouldn't like to be in their place. Not this time, at least.

If only it had been a little sooner. When Seryoga crawled into the smashed APC.

But money's money, and money's what split them up. Their partnership flushed right down the tubes, and I had to buy a little more vodka than usual a time or two.

Because they drank like horses. They would pull in from that Fryazino of theirs and drink up what I'd bought for myself. But always separately. They actually called ahead to make sure they weren't going to run into each other at my place. But I drank with them both. I didn't care who'd stiffed who. For me they would always be Pashka and Genka, the guys I burned up with. Who knew I once had a face and not this hunk of charred flesh.

Half a year after being drafted and then another whole month in Chechnya.

It was Genka who had the bright idea of getting me into Euro renovations.

"What's the big sweat?" he said to me. "Fuck, you're a carpenter. You know all that construction shit. Why don't you trick out my apartment? I can pay pretty well, and then maybe you'll find some more clients."

And I did. In several towns even. True, they were always surprised when I told them on the phone that I worked alone, but later, when they met me, they weren't surprised anymore. At least they didn't ask me why the renovations took so long. The ones who were in a hurry hired other people.

So did the ones who didn't like my face.

– – –

"Look at your faces!" the head teacher would shout at us during drafting class. "Just look at yourselves. There's not a single idea in your eyes. I might as well have a flock of sheep sitting in front of me. You're as dumb as sheep. Idiots!"

He was standing beside me, brandishing my drawing. The piece of paper was trembling in his hand, over my head. I was looking at my desk and counting the drops of spit. First one, then another. I moved back to keep from getting hit, and then he paused. He looked at me, sighed, folded the paper in half, and said, "Let's pay the director a visit. Take your things."

And he looked at all of us again.

"Everyone else, keep working. Don't even think about leaving the room."

"Take a gander at what your pupils are doing, Alexander Stepanovich," he said when we entered the director's office. "Future builders!"

"They're all our pupils, Arkady Andreyevich," the director said. "And they may never be builders."

My teacher dropped my drawing on his desk and stared at me silently. But I was looking at the director. Because I'd never seen him before. None of us ever had. The head teacher ran everything at the school, and people said all kinds of things about the director.

"Why are you looking at me like that?" He chuckled. "Am I fat? You never saw Morgunov. There was that movie once, you know? About Morgunov, Vitsin, and Nikulin."

The head teacher shuddered and started talking.

"Excuse me, Alexander Stepanovich, but it seems to me—"

"Thank you for the heads up, Arkady Andreyevich," the director interrupted him. "I'll sort this out. He can stay here in my office."

When the head teacher left, the director set my drawing aside and looked at me again.

"Well then, let's get started. Take that chair over there and sit a little closer. Otherwise I can't see at all. That's it. Good boy. Now, tell me your name."

"Konstantin."

"Konstantin? A fine name. You must be a constant person. That's good. Are you a constant person, Konstantin? Or is that just your name?"

"I don't know," I said.

I found it odd that we were sitting there like this, in his office, and he was asking me these weird questions. Because I was waiting for him to start hollering.

"You don't know? You should. You should know as much as possible about yourself, Konstantin. What do you know about yourself?"

I looked at him and didn't know what to say.

"Fine," he said. "You're not ready yet. Later, maybe, I'll ask again. Think about it. For now, though, tell me, what do you know about your bag?"

I looked at him and had no idea what he was talking about.

"Give it to me."

I handed him the bag across his desk. He took it, hefted it, and smiled.

"It's heavy. What do you have here?"

"Textbooks. And my gym uniform. We're playing basketball today."

"Good. What else?"

"Notebooks."

"What else?"

"Pens."

"Good boy. What else?"

"Nothing else."

I wondered whether I had left my cigarettes there.

He put my bag on his desk and picked up my drawing again.

"Do you have others? There, in your bag?"

I stared at him.

"Drawings, you mean?"

"Well, yes, drawings. That is why you were brought here. Any more? Show me. Or do you want me to dig around in your gym uniform?"

He spent about five minutes paging through my notebooks. Then he stood up, walked to the window, stood there, came back, and looked for another five minutes. After that he pushed it all aside and said, "Why don't you have anything besides naked women? Are you preoccupied? How old are you?"

"Sixteen."

"Ah, that explains it," he said. "Put it all back, sit over there by the wall, and wait a minute. I have a few things to finish up here."

– – –

The first time it doesn't work out right, not because you don't have any experience but because you've been waiting too long. I mean, a few years go by from the moment you start thinking about it. And the point is not that all of a sudden you end up alone with her and you kinda look at her and think, Damn, I don't have any experience.

No, it's just that you've been waiting too long. That's why it doesn't work out right. And of course, she's got the same problems. Or don't girls think about things like that?

In short, you end up starting to draw. First the neck, then the shoulder. That's how it happens. You're sitting there, mad at them, and drawing. Then you get a new notebook. And then another.

I never was able to explain to Mama where I was hanging out after class. I couldn't tell her about these drawings or about how the school director kept me after class in his office for three hours, and then he wouldn't let me go anywhere anyway and instead took me home with him. Along the way, he gave all the homeless guys money and then gave out more in front of his building; there was a whole crowd waiting for him. Maybe not a crowd, but several people. And when we went up to the third floor, some old woman was sitting on the stairs, and the director said to her, Certainly, certainly, let's go, come in, I've been expecting you for a long time. There's an awful lot piled up in the kitchen. She rattled around in the kitchen for a long time and then left. On her back was a huge knapsack with empty bottles, and the director said, That's not too heavy? Can you manage alone?

Will you make it? And the old lady said, I'll make it. Then he got out some book, showed it to me, and asked, Did you copy your drawings from here? I said, No. Because I didn't copy them. I just drew whatever came into my head. When I felt lousy. And he said, Are you sure they're not from here? And I said, No. Then he gave me the book and said, Take it home and look at it. Come here in the morning, at about eleven. I said I had a test in the morning and the head teacher would kill me. And the director said, He won't kill you. Go home and look at the book.

But I got home late anyway, and Mama really started laying into me. I looked at her and couldn't explain anything. Because I had that book in my bag. I couldn't show her that book! There were drawings in there she wouldn't have liked at all.

But Eduard Mikhailovich did. Or didn't. I don't know. But he was interested. He grabbed that book off my desk right away, the moment he walked into my room, and started leafing through it. He got this expression on his face...A weird one. And he said, Why are you making your mother crazy? Full of himself, such a concerned new father. He leafed through this book and said, Your mother nearly went out of her mind waiting for you. She was getting ready to call the police. What's this book you have? I said, You're holding it. Look at the cover. That says it all.

He said, Goya, *Caprichos*. What is this, some artist? I said, I don't know. The director gave me the book. And he said, Well, look out. You've got to quit making your mother crazy.

I looked at him and thought, Why don't you look out? If it weren't for you, I might have drawn all these dames differently. Not all misshapen.

Because it was true, they always did turn out misshapen. But I liked drawing them. You sit there and draw, and it seems to make things a little easier.

– – –

But this Eduard Mikhailovich already had me plenty irritated by then. I even refused to dodge the draft afterward because of him. Even though lots did. But by then he had me good and irritated.

He would drop into my room, sit down, and talk. He was always talking about what a jerk my father was when they were cadets in the same company. And about how foolishly Mama had behaved in marrying him. Because my father kept running around on her, and even when she was pregnant he was making out with these other girls right under her window. When she had me, he was always disappearing somewhere, too. Once she went to see them at the company and said she had nothing to feed me. I was two years old at the time. And we had no idea where my father was. And how they had all taken up a collection and fed the poor, hungry boy. And how afterward they'd beaten my father to a pulp. Or rather, they'd wanted to but he was already company commander and he'd said, Sure, go ahead. So they didn't. And in general about how thoroughly rotten he was.

But Eduard Mikhailovich was good. Because he didn't abandon my mama in her time of need. And when she was left on her own, he immediately answered the call, ready to help. Even though she already had this little numbskull.

Eduard Mikhailovich was also very smart. Because he was the first to realize where all this perestroika was leading and who this Gorbachev was and who needed all this privatization. That's why he quit the army in the nick of time. The ones who stayed behind were all utter morons. And the American president was an idiot.

Listening to Eduard Mikhailovich was pure pleasure. But I sat there in silence. Although I had to do my homework. Because Mama asked me to help her. And I did. I sat and watched him dig around in my desk. I don't know what he was searching for there. That's probably what they taught them in the army.

He also wrote letters to the editor. To all the newspapers he could buy. And to the TV station. And we had to listen to him. One day we were packing up to go mushroom hunting in the woods, but he saw something on the TV and sat right down and started writing.

We circled around him getting ready. Because there was only one bus before midday. Then you had to wait until three forty-five. But he kicked up a fuss, so Mama said, Come on, Kostya, let's listen to him. So we sat in front of him with our boots and jackets on.

And he kept saying, "Don't you realize, Svetlana, what fools they are there? Don't you?"

– – –

The refrigerator was empty seven days after I took the mirror to Olga's. Or eight. It's hard to know things like that for certain.

I gathered my strength and moved everything on the floor and windowsills into it. I don't like my vodka warm.

The first time I saw that much vodka in one place was at the director's, Alexander Stepanovich's. He never bought it by the bottle. He had an agreement with some guys to bring it a case at a time. So he wouldn't have to keep running back and forth.

"I have a terrible thirst," he would say. "An endless thirst, Konstantin. My body craves liquids. Or something else. You know, I grew up in a place where there wasn't any water at all. Not a stream or a lake. I don't even remember a proper puddle. And it almost never rained. That's why to this day I'm thirsty. I have this dried-out feeling all the time. Hand me that glass over there."

He put empty bottles, dishes, and odd shoes in front of me, and I drew. While he drank his vodka.

I liked going to his place. They forgot about me at school, and eventually the head teacher stopped marking my absences. My classmates came to see me a few times and asked me how I was doing. But I always said everything was fine and that the director and I were working on my graduation project.

I liked the fact that he drank his vodka completely differently from other men. My father always stood there for a long time with a shot glass in one hand and a glass of water in the other. He would prepare himself, gather his courage. Then he would curl his lips into a tube, shut his eyes, and slowly suck down the vodka. Eduard Mikhailovich always shuddered, as if someone had slipped a frog down his shirt.

But the director didn't drink from shot glasses at all. He poured his vodka into a tumbler and drank from it as if he really were drinking water. As if he were simply thirsty. Like someone whose throat had dried out.

He drank glass after glass, never exhaling afterward, looked at my drawings, and didn't get drunk. He just sat opposite me in his armchair and told me not to get any ideas.

Not that I was. For me, this was all just playing hooky. You leave the house and everyone thinks you've gone off to class. Or they don't. I don't know.

Because by then my mother had obviously washed her hands of me. She was camped out around her Eduard Mikhailovich. And I was angry at my father for putting me in this position. Couldn't he have let this Uncle Edik have it just once there, in their company, so that he would forget about Mama? There had to be some other decent cadets there.

In short, I didn't give my drawings much thought. What was so special about them? They have drawings in Africa, too. Anyway, mostly I hung out with my pals in the courtyard.

We chased girls, played guitar, drank sweet wine sometimes. Then we'd go watch them dismantling the enlistment office.

You're standing on the ruins, smoking and thinking, Here's where I sat naked at the military service commission. It was pretty hilarious how my butt stuck to that couch. And now it's like, That's it, evil doesn't exist anymore. And it feels really funky. Like somebody wasted Koshchei the Undead. But later it turns out to have been pointless, though. They built a new enlistment office on the next block over. This time it wasn't built of wood, though. It's like the fairytale, where you wipe out old Koshchei and he just gets tougher. You can't ever totally waste him.

That's how Genka used to talk in the war. I learned how to talk like that from him.

"Let's waste them, guys. Why the long faces? Got the willies?"

He climbed into the APC and laughed. He tapped his helmet with the loaded magazine.

"Don't piss your pants. It'll all be fine. Come on, I'll sit over here. Come on, come on, move your ass."

And he sat in my place. But I didn't care. After all, no one knew the grenade was going to burn through the armor right where he'd moved me.

– – –

And then Alexander Stepanovich would get angry for no reason at all.

"You're not paying attention," he would say. "Just because you know how to draw doesn't mean a thing. An artist has to know how to see. Look out the window. Tell me, what do you see there?"

"I'm not an artist," I said.

Then he took the boot I was drawing off the table and threw it at me.

"I told you to go over to the window!"

So I did. Because I didn't feel like sitting in class with our head teacher. It's better to dodge a boot than to pretend you don't notice spit flying from someone in all directions. He should get new teeth. Or shoot himself.

"What do you see there?"

"Nothing. I see trees and birds. Some kids on the swings."

"What are they doing?"

"Swinging. What else?"

"What are they like?"

I tried to get a better look at them.

"Ordinary. Regular children. The usual small fry."

"You're the usual small fry. Go into the kitchen. Bring me another one."

In the time it took me to walk to the refrigerator, he finished his glass.

"There's a good boy. Put it here. My God, why am I so fat? Give it to me. Can't you see I haven't finished? Sit next to me. You don't have to draw anymore."

I sat down. He opened the bottle of vodka with his teeth, poured himself a new glass, looked at it, smiled, took a few slow sips, and then leaned back in his chair with a sigh.

"Wouldn't you know it! I need something to drink. My throat is all dried out. What were you saying there about those children?"

"I said, the usual small fry."

He chuckled and gave me a disdainful look.

"There's no such thing as usual small fry, Konstantin. The people who came up with the idea of usual small fry are fools. Understand?"

"No," I said.

"Someday you will. For now just listen. Every day you walk past those children and you don't have any idea what they're like. For instance, can you tell me how one child attracts another child's attention when he wants to say something? No? He turns his head with his hands. He takes him by the face and turns it toward him with his little hands."

He looked at his own pudgy hands, sighed, and demonstrated in the air how one child turned another child's face.

"Or they draw on each other with colored markers. You can't see from here what they're drawing, but you can tell they like it. Because it tickles and they show each other what's drawn on them. Have you ever seen how a ray of light falls into a dark room from a door that's ajar? At the very beginning it's narrow, and then it spreads. It's just like a person. First he's by himself, then there are two children, then four grandchildren. Do you see? A person spreads like a ray of light. Ad infinitum. Do you see?"

He looked at me and waited for me to nod.

"Smart boy! Now tell me what you yourself did when you were little."

"I don't remember."

"Try."

"The same as everybody else."

"Played, went for walks, sat on the potty?"

"Yeah."

"Not enough. An artist has to know more."

"I'm not an artist."

"Give me that boot over there. It's too hard for me to get up."

"The least thing and damn, right away, you throw the boot."

"Don't start making faces! I'm talking to you. Come on, think."

"I don't remember anymore…I spied on the girls in kindergarten when they were peeing."

"That's better. What else?"

"I waited for my mama. She always came after everyone else."

"Not bad."

"I sat in my classroom and looked out the window. And the teacher's aide said I'd really got her goat with that mama of mine."

"What was she like?"

"Tall. I don't remember. She had this thick plaid skirt. Once I went into the back room and she was standing there in her slip. My mama had the same one. She leaned over and slapped me in the face. But I'd just walked in. My ball had rolled in there. I didn't have anyone to play with."

"Did you hate her?"

"I don't know. Probably. Mama said her husband had been killed in Afghanistan. He was an officer."

– – –

When they brought new guys, Genka would always ask them who they were and where they were from. He said we Muscovites had to stick together. Let the hicks check out alone. He himself was from Fryazino. Pashka had been called up from there, too. Genka said they were lucky. They walked out of the same enlistment office, went through basic together, and ended up here in the same unit. It doesn't always happen that way. And I was from Podolsk. So when Seryoga showed up, Genka told him straightaway, Have no fear. There are already a good three of us here. We won't let you down. Because Seryoga really was from Moscow. He'd lived his whole life at 3 Eighth of March Street. Ten minutes by bus to the Metro. A Dinamo fan, naturally.

"Yeah, that team of yours!" Genka said. "They still can't play for shit. Tell him, Pashka. Can they play for shit?"

Pashka didn't say anything. Because he rarely spoke anyway. He went everywhere with Genka, but he himself almost never spoke. He would shrug and shift his submachine gun.

"How's about it, soldier?" Genka said to Seryoga. "Stick with us. Otherwise they're gonna blow your ass off, and then you'll be sorry."

But we didn't fight as a foursome for long. When we got into the APC that morning, Genka laughed at Seryoga.

"Fuck, soldier! We've all been the FNG. What did you expect? You'd go to war and not find out what an FNG was? Pashka over there, his father was in the navy. In the beginning they had him sharpening the anchor. So it would slip into the bottom better. Can you imagine? With files. Tell him, Pashka."

Seryoga climbed into the APC last and shut the hatch.

"Too bad they didn't take me into the navy. I'd have sharpened a hundred anchors for them."

"Not to worry, soldier," Genka said. "There's no escaping your fate. Six months ago they brought in a whole detachment of dirt sailors. They were probably happy when they were called up, too. Like, we're gonna sail the seven seas. But you shouldn't have shut the hatch, soldier."

"Why?"

"Because you're riding with me. If you were riding alone, no one would have said a damn word."

"I don't get it."

"You will when a grenade lands in the tank. It'll burn through the fucking armor and blow up inside. And it'll blast us all to smithereens because the pressure in a closed space is a whole different thing. Ever study physics, soldier? Or did you spend your whole time jacking off in the school toilet? Come on, Kostya, let me sit over here. Come on, come on, move your ass. And you, soldier, open the hatch. What are you staring at?"

– – –

To be honest, I don't know why I drew him drunk. Maybe because by that time there was nothing else to draw. I'd already drawn everything at Alexander Stepanovich's. All his shoes, dishes, bottles, books, and stupid figurines. Everything he put in front of me. There was nothing left to draw. And it's pretty boring just sitting around. Because he was in a drunken stupor and I was sitting facing him, not knowing how to leave. There wasn't anyone to close the door behind me.

That's why, when I came in one day and this guy was in my room—well, naturally, I got a little embarrassed. Eduard Mikhailovich told me, This is Alexander Stepanovich's son, and while he was talking he was looking at me so oddly, as if I'd invited him. I stepped into my room and saw him holding that drawing of mine, because like a fool I'd left it on my desk. I'd wanted Eduard Mikhailovich to find it and get all worked up. I liked razzing him. But now I was just standing in front of this guy, and I didn't know what to do. Because who would like it if someone drew their father looking like that? I mean, when he's in a drunken stupor, basically sprawled out in his apartment like who knows fucking what?

But he just said his name was Boris Alexandrovich and that he had come to have a little chat with me. We sat down by my desk and started talking. But he held onto the drawing. And asked about Alexander Stepanovich. He said the head teacher had given him my address because he wanted to talk to me personally. About his father, and all the rest in general. At first I told him everything seemed OK to me, but I couldn't give him this total bunch of malarkey and say something like, Alexander Stepanovich doesn't drink at all. He was holding my drawing in the first place. He asked whether it was a lot in a day and how often. And I said, Constantly. Two or three bottles, but sometimes even more. Depending on his mood. That made him sad. I told him he shouldn't be upset because Alexander Stepanovich was a smart guy and told me all kinds of interesting things. But for some reason that made him even sadder. He said he wanted to take him home with him to the Krasnodar area because it was nice there and close to the sea. But Alexander Stepanovich had no intention of leaving. He said he should go back to his little Gostagayevo without him. And that he'd always been a little odd. He could be working in a ministry in Moscow right now, and instead he was sitting around here drinking vodka. And that many years ago he could have become a great artist—as good as Glazunov—and the whole family could have been living abroad a long time ago, but he gave up painting, and after

that gave up architecture, even though he had a building right in downtown Moscow, and his friend became a
minister only because Alexander Stepanovich had done
these projects for him and he hadn't even asked for anything in return, because he'd said he didn't need anything, he already had everything. In short, I was sitting
in my room listening to him, not knowing why he was
telling me all this, but he was talking and talking, all the
while looking at my drawing. Then he finally stopped
talking, and I could hear Eduard Mikhailovich read-
ing Mama his new letter for *Arguments and Facts*. But
Boris Alexandrovich obviously didn't hear it. Because he
was engrossed in his own thoughts and just sat there in
silence.

Then he took another look at the drawing and said,
"It's because of you that he doesn't want to leave. He's
never had a pupil like you before."

– – –

The next day Alexander Stepanovich immediately
demanded the drawing. I said I'd lost it, and he shouted,
I'm going to send you back to class! Then I showed it to
him, and for a long time he sat there without moving a
muscle.

Then he sighed and said, "Borka wasn't lying after
all. I thought he was sucking up to me."

After that he looked up.

"So, you do know how to see after all. You calculated the perspective yourself, too."

"I didn't calculate anything."

"Quiet! Why don't you tell me when the last time was you went to class?"

"Me?"

"Stop acting the fool with me."

"Two days ago."

"What for?"

"I had to pay a guy back."

"So how was it there?"

"OK."

"Did you see Arkady Andreyevich?"

"Who?"

"The head teacher. What, have you decided to tick me off especially today?"

"No, it's true, I forgot his name. We call him the camel."

"He spits?" Alexander Stepanovich chuckled, and his body started swaying like a giant balloon.

"And how!"

"I see. That one's going to spit far eventually. Well, did you see him or not?"

"Yes."

"What did he say to you?"

"Nothing. He asked about you."

"What did you tell him?"

"I said you were sick."

"Sick? You're a fool! You have to tell him the truth. Otherwise he's going to eat you alive. Especially when he becomes director."

I never forgot our head teacher's name again. Because Alexander Stepanovich was right. Arkady Andreyevich really did become director. I don't know—maybe his friend the minister was transferred or Alexander Stepanovich himself decided homemade wines would do a better job of slaking his thirst. My father used to tell me when I was a kid that there's a good southern wine called Massandra. I don't know why I remembered what it was called. I thought it must taste even better than ice cream. Maybe the director went to his son's so he could drink that wine. I don't know. He told me not to give up drawing. Otherwise he'd come back and personally rip my head off. Actually, the word he used was noggin.

"Get what I'm saying? God forbid you give it up. I won't just rip your noggin off then."

But he never did come. I stopped drawing almost immediately after because I was hoping he'd been telling me the truth. I waited for him a few more months. But it turned out to be a load of crap. He probably didn't even remember my name.

Arkady Andreyevich wasted no time getting started on my education. That's why, as soon as my call-up papers came, I was the first to head for the enlistment office. After all, nobody knew how it was all going to end. Especially since I was thoroughly fed up with Eduard Mikhailovich.

– – –

"Listen, Kostya!" Genka shouted right in my ear when the APC started moving. "You want us to pay your stepdad a visit after demob and rip off his balls? Hey, Pashka? Wanna rip that jerk's balls off?"

I shook my head because I didn't feel like shouting over the noise of the engine. Not only that, this weird captain from division headquarters was riding with us. And also an ensign, Demidov, who had never gotten into an APC with us before.

Genka looked in their direction as well and then leaned toward me and hollered in my ear again.

"Crummy spies! Damn! They're paying a call on the Chechens, to divvy up the spoils—who gets how much if we don't bomb Staropromyslovsky. They've got those crappy oil rigs there."

I looked toward the captain, but he could hardly have heard Genka; he was sitting too far away. Ensign Demidov was listening to his trophy cassette player. Two days before, the boys had captured a sniper and thrown him off the fifth floor. They gave his player to Demidov. He was a good person to have on your side. Before the war he'd worked as a supplier.

"How's about it, soldier?" Genka shouted at Seryoga. "How long are you gonna fuck around with that hatch?"

"It doesn't want to open."

Seryoga was tugging at the handle as hard as he could.

"Move the fuck over! Look. This is how you do it. See?"

Genka opened the hatch and started laughing at Seryoga again.

"You're fucking hopeless. Look, they're going to shoot you you-know-where, and then what'll you go home with? What are you going to bang your women with, your rifle butt? Hey! Don't sit there. Come here. Stick your head out the hatch."

Seryoga looked at him as if he were a ghost.

"What are you goggling at? Come on, get out there, do as you're told."

"There're snipers out there."

"So what? You wanted to sit in here? Go on, crawl on out. I'm talking to you. We're just about to pass the ruins. The spooks sit there all the time with their bumblebees. If a grenade lands in the APC, at least it'll throw you out alive. Then you can come back and pull us out. See? Whoever's moving, pull them out first. Got it? Up you go."

Seryoga stuck his head out the hatch and fell tensely still. Genka went over to the lookout slit.

"We're coming up on the ruins!" he shouted into the two-way. "Hear me? Have you fucking fallen asleep there? We're getting closer. Cover us if anything happens. Two hundred meters to go. A hundred fifty. A hundred. All's well. No one's there, I think. Fifty meters to go. Nearly past. All's quiet here. What? No, all's well, I said. It's quiet here, quiet—"

– – –

The explosion was so loud I jumped to my feet. Jumped up and fell straight down. My head was ringing from the blow, like being inside a bell. There was an empty bottle in front of my eyes. And another one next to it. I touched them and they clinked. Lying on the floor felt good. The floor was cool. I pressed my cheek to the linoleum and shut my eyes. Just so I didn't move…

At that moment someone started banging on the door again. More like kicking. Right at my head.

I sat up, opened my eyes, and started getting up very slowly. The main thing was not to make any sudden movements. So it wouldn't explode. Because it would be very hard to clean up. I wouldn't be able to bend over more than once.

They started beating on the door again. What's the big rush? Do they think I'm an express train?

They can go to hell, anyone who comes see you in the middle of the night and kicks at your door. What time is it anyway? What day is it?

I hope their legs fall off.

"Hello!" Genka said when I opened the door. "You look like hell, dude."

I was about to check the mirror, but then I remembered I'd taken it to Olga's ten days ago. Or twelve.

"My, this is quite a disaster zone you've got here!" he said as he walked into the room. "The patient is more dead than alive. And I'm thinking, why aren't you opening the door?"

"Sit over there."

"Oh no, Commander. I'd rather stand. My wife just bought me these jeans."

"Get out!" I said, dropping back down to the floor.

"What's the matter, are you totally wasted?"

"Leave me alone, I'm telling you. Can't you see I feel rotten?"

"Yeah. Been at it long?"

"I don't know. A couple of weeks. What day is it? Why did you come in the middle of the night anyway? It is night now, right?"

"You're amazing, Commander! It's nine o'clock in the evening. I've been trying to reach you for two days, by the way. What's with your phone?"

He leaned over the jack and picked up the disconnected line.

"I see. Fed up with the outside world?"

"Get out."

"Yesterday I called your neighbor, Svetlana."

"Olga."

"Like I care. She said you were on a binge. She knocked at your door. She says there's no point."

"I didn't hear her."

"That's putting it mildly. I nearly banged my fists off myself. So, let us arise and get you cleaned up. I'm spending the night with you, and tomorrow we'll pick up Pashka and go to Moscow. His car's not running, and he won't ride in the same SUV with me without you. You know about that whole mess."

I could barely raise my head.

"Why the fuck should we go to Moscow? Have you two decided to make up or something?"

He stared at me and for a few seconds said nothing.

"You really are something! Don't you know anything at all? Didn't Pashka call you? When did you disconnect the phone? You mean he didn't call you?"

I rose partway and sat up on the floor in front of him. My head was ringing like the bells at Easter.

"Someone called but I didn't talk. My head hurt too bad."

"You're something. Seryoga's gone missing, and you don't know a damn thing. Tomorrow we're going out looking for him. Got any vodka left?"

– – –

This wasn't the first time Seryoga'd gone missing. After demob nothing ever panned out for him really. Not like for Pashka or me. To say nothing of Genka. In the beginning we tried to help. We found him a job. Then another. Then Genka said he was done meeting with those people. Like, they'd trusted him, and he'd stuck them with Seryoga. But he wanted to make deals with them for big bucks. Which is why we just started giving Seryoga money. First me, then Pashka. Genka would give him money, too. But it was pointless. You could give Seryoga a hundred rubles or two hundred bucks, and it would all vanish at one go. Nothing ever panned out for him.

At first the guys around him seemed OK. Sit around, have a drink—How ya doin'? Later, though, these homeless guys started showing up. Because he had an apartment. And he lived alone. At first his aunt put up a fight, but before long she bought a house in Kaluga Province and told him, I'm sorry, I'm getting old and I don't need this kind of headache. And he just couldn't get in a job groove. First it was one thing, then another. Either his boss was an asshole or it was a crappy job. Something always went wrong. The last time Pashka and I dragged him out of a real hole. He was sleeping at Domodedovo Airport. In a room full of tombstones.

So this was nothing new. But Genka said that Seryoga's aunt was beside herself. She'd called him a few times and cried the whole time. Someone she knew had gone to Moscow and told her that these other people were living in Seryoga's apartment. They didn't want to talk about him and wouldn't open the door.

"Basically, she won't let go of the idea that Seryoga's been killed. She's losing her mind in her old age. These old farts are always imagining fuck-all. That garden's driven the old lady batty. She's probably growing marijuana to sell."

"Maybe we should go see her first," I said. "When did she last see him?"

"Enough already! Cut it out! Tomorrow we're going to Moscow. I said, where do you keep the vodka? There's zilch left in the fridge."

– – –

We got to Fryazino a little before eleven. The weather was lousy so we drove slowly. First rain, then snow. A few times we just plain had to stop.

At Pashka's house Genka handed me his phone.

"Tell him to move his buns."

Five minutes later Pashka climbed in the back without a word, slapped me on the shoulder, and started staring out the window. As if he'd never seen his own yard before. Never in his life.

"How's the family?" I turned to face him across the seat.

He shrugged in reply.

This money business had created a lot of tension for them. He and Genka had actually decided to split up the business. They'd stopped seeing each other altogether and started drinking vodka with different people. Although, how could they get away from each other in Fryazino? All the people were the same people. So they had to check ahead of time, to make sure they didn't meet somewhere by accident. Who knew how that might end? Pashka didn't like to talk, but he could drink an awful lot of vodka at one go. Two bottles. Three, even, if he was in the mood.

From what I could tell from their drunken stories, things had gone to hell over fifty thou. A lot of money, sure, but was it worth that? They'd come to see me later, rocking on the footstool and repeating over and over, You know perfectly well I couldn't abandon him. You know that, don't you? Say it.

I needed these conversations like a hole in the head. Because neither one of them could calm down. They'd come see me and drink my vodka. But the real joke was that I really didn't know which one of them had taken the loot.

Originally they'd been going to buy themselves a couple of houses somewhere abroad. Because the money was rolling in, raining down on them, like no one had ever expected. This one business had turned out that well. But later they found out that fifty thou isn't enough for two houses, just for one. So they decided to put it off: you know, we'll think of something later. But when "later" came the money wasn't there. And each of them was saying he wasn't the one who took it. Pashka's wife went to Genka's house to talk about something. Genka didn't want to discuss the encounter with me, and when Pashka was drunk, he just ground his teeth. Another idiotic habit.

In short, the story was shit. The same old fucking shit.

That's why Pashka was looking out the window at his hometown of Fryazino. With deep and abiding interest. And Genka was driving the SUV as if he were taking his driver's test. And I was next to him like some driving instructor. Except that I can't even drive a car. And I didn't really find the Fryazino out my window particularly thrilling.

"What's this you have?" I said, picking up a small blue-bound book off the floor.

"Some bozo gave it to me," said Genka. "Some American missionary. He was ordering some furniture from us for his chapel."

At the word *us* he tore his eyes away from the road for the first time since Pashka'd gotten into the SUV and looked back. Maybe not exactly looked, but shifted in that direction.

I opened the book in the middle and read the first thing my eyes came across: "Then entered Satan into Judas surnamed Iscariot, being of the number of the twelve."

"Toss it in there." Genka reached across and opened the glove compartment. "I have to give it to my wife. She's into that drivel lately."

"Just a sec," I said. "Let me take another look."

– – –

Once when I was a kid my father told me, Don't read too much. You'll ruin your eyes. But I never did read too much. And I didn't read too little either. I'd just happened to pick up the book he'd seen me with then. It was Mama's book on how to crochet. Hooks and loops and whatnot. I don't know why I even opened it. Boredom, probably. And right then my father comes up. And he says, Don't read too much.

It was the same story with the bicycle. And with teaching me to score a goal. As if there were no such thing. No bike, no ball, no knee. No me, either. But there were the neighbor kids. At least each of them had a father holding onto his bike. Standing behind and holding onto the rack. Then they'd ask me if I wanted them to hold me. But I always said they didn't have to. Because it's better like that, when you're all on your own. You come home and rub your bruises with a soup spoon. And your father rustles his newspaper, looks at you, and says to be sure to wash it afterward.

That's why when no one opened the door at Seryoga's apartment and Genka said that evidently we were going to have to go see my father, I just stood there in that dirty entryway next to the green wall dumbfounded, looking at him, at a loss for words.

"Well, what are you staring at?" he said. "Why don't you say something? You were the one who said when you were drunk that he works at Moscow City Hall. Let's go see him and have a chat. He can find out there about the apartment sale. Who bought it and when. There ought to be some office there, too, about those homeless guys. Registration…you know, what to do and where to go. Let's go. Time fucking waits for no man."

"I haven't seen him in ten years."

"So what? Now you will. Cut the pity party! Without him, no one's going to give us any information about Seryoga's apartment. And without that information we might as well butt out altogether. We have to find out who's living there. And how they fucking got there. Come on, out with the address."

I looked at Pashka, but he had just that moment turned away.

– – –

"Who do you want?" the young woman said as she opened the door.

She was frightened. You could hear it in her voice. We were standing in front of her like three wise guys. I tried to hide behind Genka a little. Just because of my face.

"Oh, it's you, Kostya!" said my father, who loomed up in the hallway behind her. "Come on in, boys. Everyone come in."

I took a step from behind Genka's back, and my father embraced me in his strong arms.

"Here you've come at last. I've been waiting for this for a long time."

– – –

The vodka he had was expensive. With import labels and an attractive bottle. But there wasn't much. Only enough for fifteen minutes.

"Marina, go buy us a little more vodka," my father said. "Or else pretty soon everyone here's going to die of thirst."

"You've got a meeting tomorrow," she said, trying not to look in my direction.

"I remember. Go out and buy some, precious. My son and I need to drink some vodka finally. What took you so long to come? Eh, Kostya?"

"I had things to do," I said.

"I've been wanting to show you your brother and sister. Do you know about them? Of course, they're in school right now. Natashka's in fifth and Slavka's started first. Both on the second shift. You know, they're so funny."

"I can imagine."

"Oh, you have no idea. Tell me, how are you doing?"

He looked me in the face, which wasn't easy for him to do, I could tell.

"You can see for yourself."

"Enough of that! You never know what life will bring. The main thing is you're alive."

He paused and twirled his empty glass in his hands.

"But in general, how are you doing? Has it been hard?"

"It hasn't been easy."

"I realize that. But how did it happen?"

"They chucked a bumblebee into our APC."

"And these boys were with you?" He looked at Genka and Pashka.

"They were taken out before. Seryoga thought I was dead."

My father paused again; then he sighed deeply and tore his eyes from his empty glass.

"As for your Seryoga, to be honest, I don't know how I can help you. I'm in a completely different department. I do patriotic education."

"You mean military training in the schools?" said Genka.

"Among other things."

"I get it. Zarnitsa war games. All that crap."

"It's not crap," my father said, and he placed his glass on the table. "We have to raise the army's prestige."

"And what's your rank?"

"Lieutenant colonel."

"Not bad! Did you fight, too? Any hot spots? Afghanistan?"

My father looked at Genka, and his eyes almost narrowed.

"No, I never had to. I work in personnel."

"I see. End of questions."

"Here's your vodka," Marina said as she came into the kitchen. "You can drink to your hearts' content."

"No, thanks," Genka said. "We'd better be on our way. There's a lot of vodka anywhere else. And we have to be back in Moscow bright and early. We're still going to give our all trying to find him. Have a nice day, Comrade Lieutenant Colonel. Now I understand why Kostya didn't want to see you."

In the hall, nearly to the door, Marina suddenly spoke up.

"But if you're coming back to Moscow tomorrow, maybe Konstantin could stay here and spend the night. Why drive back and forth? We have a spare room."

"No, thanks," I said. "I need to get to Podolsk. I have something important to attend to."

Downstairs Genka got in the SUV and started the motor but for some reason was in no hurry to get going. "Listen!" He turned to me at last. "You know what? Why don't you stay? Why the fuck should we drive you to Podolsk? It means an extra hour and a half on the road. Tomorrow we'll come by for you at eleven. He is your father. Come on, bro, clear out."

– – –

"Here's your room," Marina said, letting me go ahead. "Make yourself comfortable. Meanwhile, Nikolai will bring the children home from school. It's very close. Next door. Right in our courtyard."

It felt a little strange, her calling my father Nikolai. My mother always called him by his last name. As if he were a classmate. Or a politician in the newspapers.

"I was the one who hung this here," she said, noticing my glance. "I love Armenian painting. I don't know who did it, of course, but the landscape is obviously Erevan. See, here you have the characteristic stormy tones, and here are the little houses climbing uphill. I spent my childhood in Erevan. It's very beautiful there."

"It's an El Greco," I said.

"What?"

"It's a reproduction of a painting by El Greco. A Spanish artist. Of Greek descent. His real name was Dominico Theotocopuli. Not that it matters."

She shifted her gaze toward me. There was surprise in her eyes.

"You're certain?"

"Yes."

I looked at her and thought, What did my mother lack to compete with her?

"Well, if you think so…"

Her voice held an abyss of doubt.

"I don't think so. It's an El Greco."

She looked at me again and finally smiled.

"Fine. If it's El Greco, it's El Greco. What's the difference really? You know, don't be mad at your father. He has a very difficult situation at work right now. Maybe I can help you in some way."

"You?"

"Yes. I have reporter friends who work the crime beat. They have great connections with the Moscow police."

I was about to say that wouldn't be bad, but right then the doorbell rang.

"Our family's back," she said. "Come on, I'll introduce you."

The little girl wouldn't even look at me. She whispered, "'Lo," and slipped off to her room. My father had obviously warned them.

So they wouldn't stare.

But the boy was very little. Chubby cheeks and round eyes. He stared at me, and his lips even parted slightly. He stopped unbuttoning his jacket.

My father said, "They were both let out early. They've been throwing snowballs outside for a whole hour."

"Slavka, it's not polite to stare at people," Marina said behind my back. "Come say hello. This is your brother."

I squatted in front of him and held out my hand.

"Nice to meet you, little brother. My name is Konstantin."

His eyes got even bigger. He looked at me and then Marina. He held out his hand and finally said, "My ears froze hard as rocks. They don't bend at all."

– – –

"They're so different," Marina said when my father went to put the children to bed. "Slavka is very independent. He wants to figure everything out himself. And Natashka lives by his side like a little flower. Just so she gets a little sunlight. Though she's three years older. Here, have some sugar."

She paused for a second and smiled.

"I remember taking her to kindergarten and I was very late. We'd been putting an issue to bed, and I hadn't slept all night. But along the way Natashka asked me to stop in at the market. She wanted to buy berries."

She smiled again.

"We came running into the kindergarten very late, and the teacher started lecturing me and shouting at her. 'Why do you come so late? All the children have assembled.' You know, that strict kind of lady."

She looked at me.

"Do you mind me using the familiar 'you'?"

"That's fine."

"So. And Natashka looks and looks at her. Then she holds her hand out in front, opens it, and says, 'Bird cherries.' They had all smushed up in her fist. And she's standing there smiling."

She covered her eyes for a second.

"And this teacher is looking at her and doesn't know what to say. I'll probably remember that my whole life. Why don't you have some candy? Are you just going to drink tea?"

"I'm fine. I don't like sweets."

"That's because you like vodka. If you drink vodka you don't eat sweets. And vice versa. For instance, I can't stand the smell of it. It turns my stomach instantly. How you drink it I'll never understand."

"We drink it just fine. You just have to get used to it."

"Oh, all right," she said. "It doesn't matter. I was starting to tell you about the children. You don't mind me talking about them so much, do you?"

"That's OK. I'm interested."

"They are your brother and sister."

"Yes, I understand."

"So. But Slavka is completely different. He's so little, but he's already got a mind of his own. He's learning a few English words. And the most important thing is, no one's forcing him. He says, I need it for this computer game. It's only in English. He's also learned to play chess. Now he pesters Nikolai every day. He says he'll be beating him in a year. He's so stubborn."

She smiled again.

"And Natashka repeats everything he does like a little monkey. Though she's three years older. The other day she came up to me and asked, How does a knight go? Does the letter *l* take up two spaces or three? And of course I didn't remember myself. We had to ask Slavka."

Marina stood up and made sure the door was closed.

"True, they do fight sometimes. Rarely, but it does happen. The day before yesterday Slavka was retrieving a ball from under the bed while Natashka was walking around the room with her eyes closed. And she told him if she stepped on him it wasn't her fault. Naturally, she stepped on him immediately."

"Why have you shut yourselves in here?" my father said, peeking into the kitchen. "I thought you were watching television."

"I was afraid we were talking too loud. Pour yourself tea. I'm telling Konstantin stories about the children. Are they asleep already?"

My father looked at me and smiled.

"Yes. You know what Slavka said to me? He said, 'What incompetent boots I have. You should get me new ones.' Imagine, 'incompetent'!"

Marina laughed and fanned herself.

"A couple of years ago he woke up once and said, 'How do you pronounce a number if first there's a "one" and then an "eight"?' I said, 'Eighteen.' Then he went on. 'There are eighteen days until Christmas.' I still can't for the life of me figure out how he knew how many days were left if he couldn't say the number. But there were exactly eighteen days left."

"He was looking forward to presents," my father said. "Think of yourself as a kid before Christmas."

"Oh, that was so long ago."

I watched my own father—pouring himself tea, adding sugar to it, sitting down at the table. I watched his wife, who was looking at him and laughing, at the kitchen table with the candies under the low-hanging pink lampshade, at my own dark blue cup and the cold tea in it, at the plastic gun Slavka had left at the other end of the table. I looked at all this and strange thoughts occurred to me. Or rather, not thoughts but one thought. Not even a thought but a simple question.

Why?

I looked at them and thought, Why have things worked out for me this way? Why do some burn up and others get carried out? Why did other children end up getting the father I had? Why did the man I wanted to have for a father abandon me and go somewhere on the Black Sea? Why did that jerk who now calls himself my father affect me in such a way that I haven't had it in me to see my own mother for six whole months?

Actually, all this was probably too much for a single "why." One question mark was obviously not going to cover it.

– – –

The next morning Genka arrived alone. He said Pashka had decided to take the train. I got in beside him and we set out. For the first ten minutes he didn't say a word. This was not like Genka at all, but my mind was elsewhere. I was thinking about my new relatives.

"Damn it! Just toss it out!" He found his voice at last when he saw I had again picked up the little blue book I'd found in his car the day before.

I didn't say anything for a while and then opened it again at random: "He hath blinded their eyes, and hardened their heart; that they should not see with their eyes, nor understand with their heart, and be converted, and I should heal them."

"Hey," I said. "Why are you wearing dark glasses? It's not sunny."

Genka turned his face toward me for a second but didn't answer.

Pashka was standing by the entrance to the Metro looking straight at his feet. He was wearing dark glasses, too. As if he were blind. Except that he had on very big glasses. Like a fashion model. He might have borrowed them from his wife.

"Is this some kind of joke?" I said when he got into the SUV. "What the fuck are you wearing glasses for? It's not sunny today."

Pashka didn't reply. Genka shifted gears and stepped on the pedal.

"Wait up," I said. "Hold on. Stop the car."

"Well, what is it?" He turned to face me again.

I reached out quickly and pulled off his glasses. He had a bruise under his left eye. A deep purple bruise.

"Have you gone stupid or something?" he said, grabbing his glasses out of my hands. "Have you flipped?"

Pashka turned toward the window and wouldn't even look in my direction. No one said anything for a minute probably. Maybe even two.

"So who won?" I said finally, trying to speak softly. "Have you figured out who's tougher?"

They looked straight ahead in silence. Neither one said a word.

"You put on glasses," I continued. "You put on glasses so no one would see what you have on your faces. So everyone would think everything was fine with your face. It's just your eyes hurt. Blinded by the bright sun. So what kind of glasses am I supposed to put on, damn it? Me, damn it! On this damn face of mine!"

I didn't notice when I'd started shouting.

"What the fuck do you want with these glasses? What, are your children afraid of you? Do your wives hate looking at you? Are you the one your neighbors call in when their children don't want to go to bed? Or maybe they took your skin off along with your vest. They cut it out piece by piece because the bitch had grown right into your body. Melted there like it belonged. If you knew how sick and tired I am of your money, your silence, your faces. How sick of you I am! I don't understand what the fuck you need glasses for. What do you have to hide?"

I stopped talking. We sat there like that for about five minutes. Then Genka coughed and turned the key in the ignition.

"Well then, are we off?" he said. "What are we sitting around for? We have to look for Seryoga."

– – –

When you're a kid you fight with your friends all the time. You grapple with someone in the entryway and bang his head against a step, while upstairs the neighbors jingle their keys.

Not because you hate him but because he's always there. That's just how it is.

What do you really have left from your childhood? The dreams where you walk up to your first house and try to open the door, all the while knowing no one's there? And you're so small again and you can't reach the handle? The smells?

Or that horror in kindergarten when everyone else has fallen asleep and you've spent the whole naptime sitting on your cot because you suddenly realized you were going to die someday? Forever. And the blanket cover got all balled up and sticky because of that. And later you threw up at snack time because you shouldn't drink warm kefir after making discoveries like that. And the teacher's aide said, Take this rag and clean it up. No one's going to be wiping up after you here. Really, such a messy little boy. And you threw up again. Because you were only four. And that's not the best age to meet a woman who doesn't care about your death. But you cleaned it all up.

In short, it's not entirely clear what you have left from your childhood.

The next day they didn't come. Neither Genka nor Pashka. No one even called. I sat in a chair and started watching the children. Marina and my father left right after breakfast.

"Aren't you going to work?" Slavka said.

"No," I said. "I don't have any work right now."

"That's good." He shook his head very seriously. "Papa and Mama always have a lot of work and they don't stay with us."

"You don't have to stay with me anymore," Natashka said. "I'm going to figure skating soon."

"You're not holding the pencil right," I told Slavka. "Let me show you how it's done."

"Do you know how?" He looked at me mistrustfully. "Anyway, we're out of paper. Mama has a whole pack, but she gets mad. And Elena Viktorovna told everyone to bring a squirrel to class. Do you know how?"

There was hope in his voice. He stopped talking and stared at me.

"I don't know. Let's give it a try. Except it's better to draw on the floor. I like drawing lying down."

He readily climbed down from his chair.

"I like the floor, too. How do people draw lying down?"

"Like this," I said. "You lie on your belly and draw. See?"

Natashka looked up from her homework and watched us.

"Like this. You lie down and then you draw."

A minute later he snatched the paper from me, jumped up, and ran to his sister.

"Look, Natashka! Look how he drew!"

She got up from the table, came over to me, and dropped to the floor, too.

"Can you draw Barbie?"

"I want Pokemon!" Slavka exclaimed. "Draw Pokemon!"

I shrugged.

"I don't know what Pokemon is."

Natashka said, "Draw Barbie."

Then they asked for the Snow Queen. Then a hedgehog. Then Britney Spears and the Ninja Turtles. After that we ran out of paper and Slavka rushed to Marina's room. When he came back, he stopped for a second in the doorway, then ran toward me, holding out a whole stack of paper and a videotape, got up on tiptoe, shut his eyes, and in one exhale said, "I want the Pokemons. All of them!"

We watched cartoons and I drew. Natashka and Slavka kept running into the kitchen and bringing back chips, Coca-Cola, candy, and cheese. After a couple of hours the whole floor was littered with paper and food. When the cartoons ended, I just drew. The children watched my drawings and tried to guess what they would be. Slavka almost always guessed first.

"A hippopotamus!" he shouted, and Natashka sighed bitterly. "An ostrich! An egg! A submarine!"

So Natashka wouldn't feel so bad, I started drawing what little girls like.

"That must be a poodle," she said. "And that's a Siamese cat. And this is a teacher because she has a pointer in her hand. This must be a stewardess. But I don't know who this is. She's wearing a strange little hat."

"Who is it?" said Slavka when I finished the drawing. "We give up. Tell us, since no one can guess anyway."

"It's a surgical nurse," I said. "Her name is Anna Nikolayevna."

"What's a surgical nurse?" Slavka asked, but at that moment the lock clicked in the hall and Marina appeared in the doorway.

Astonished, she surveyed the paper-strewn room, the remains of our food, and us sitting on the floor and looking up at her, and waited a few seconds before finally speaking.

"My meal feels neglected. Did anyone at least do their homework?"

— — —

After we'd tidied up a little, Marina said that Slavka had Happy Starts that day. But she had to run to the office because some American journalist had arrived.

"*The New York Times.* Do you know that paper? I absolutely must speak to him."

I said I didn't know it but I could take Slavka instead. Genka and Pashka hadn't shown up anyway.

"It's no big deal. Just tell me how to get there."

While he was in drawing class, I sat on a bench by the school and watched people. After lunchtime the sun came out and the snow that had been falling for the last two days quickly melted. The people who were late for class ran right through the puddles. A few looked up and then noticed me. They would have been better off watching their feet. At least they wouldn't catch it later at home for their boots.

Actually, they'd be going into the army soon. Let them look.

Happy Starts was just for first graders. That's why I sat so no one could see me. With my back turned. I had to root for Slavka by ear. I listened to them shriek when someone was running in last. They were trying to help. They hollered like madmen.

"Come over here," a woman's voice spoke behind my back. "No one's here. Just some man."

Two little boys sat down on the bench opposite me. I leaned over so I wouldn't scare them. As if I were retying my shoelaces.

But they weren't interested in me.

"What do you think you're wearing?" their mama whispered. "I left everything out for you. And you put on I don't know what. Now everyone's going to think we're poor."

"Papa dressed us," one of the boys whispered. "I told him it was wrong, but he said to cut it out, we were already late."

"Now everyone's going to think you have nothing to put on. I left everything on the armchair."

"Papa said we shouldn't dress like that for Happy Starts."

"All right," the mama whispered. "Ira's running over now, and you can put on her sneakers. Only don't step in a puddle. They're brand-new."

"Then he'll come in last, if he has to run around the puddles," whispered the younger boy. "He'll lose."

"Oh, I'll jump over them."

"What if they're big?"

"I'll take a running start."

"All right, stop it," their mama's whisper cut them short. "You're making my head spin."

I listened to them, trying to be unobtrusive and thinking about how children are. What they say, how they push, how they jump with one leg tucked behind the other, how they pull off their boots, spit from the balcony, draw on the wallpaper, and fish the onions out of their soup.

Especially when they're yours.

Arriving at the Black Sea with the whole gang. In the summer, when the heat is incredible. Renting a one-room apartment. It's the second floor, so you're afraid to leave the balcony door open at night. Every hour the TV news reports about Georgians escaping from prison. Several of them. After half a bottle it's hard to remember how many. Or you don't feel like it. Especially in that heat. You have a sticky back and your thoughts are running in all directions. On the other hand, there aren't any flies. They buzz at the balcony door, but you can barely hear them in the room. Because the children are so noisy. They're shoving one another and giggling on the floor. They like being in the same room with us. You can't put them to bed. We sit on the couch and say, It's nearly two in the morning. Not that they care. They don't hear us. Their hair is wet from the heat. They grab each other's shoulders. We say, It's two o'clock. On the third day we figure out we can make our bed in the kitchen. Just on a blanket. So it doesn't hurt the knees. And so the linoleum doesn't stick to the back. The radio on the stool right over your head plays nothing but Joe Dassin every night. You have to be careful when you get up. Gasping for air, it's easy to knock it off the stool. And you'll have to find her lips in silence. As if you've gone deaf. And there's a steady roar in your head, like when you press a shell to your ear.

– – –

"Kostya! Hey, Kostya!" my father shouted to me. "Come here! Are you deaf or something? I've been calling and calling and you don't hear."

"It's noisy there on the balcony," I said, walking into the room. "Too many cars below."

"What did you expect? It's Moscow! Practically city center. Let's go have supper. Marina's home from work."

"So, didn't your friends come?" Marina said in the kitchen.

"No. They had complications. They may not come tomorrow either."

"Listen, for some reason I started using the formal 'you' with you again. What are you more comfortable with?"

"I don't care."

"Then let's use the informal. If I forget, be sure to remind me. OK? How did our Slavka do running at Happy Starts?"

She stabbed a piece of meat with a fork and knocked my father with her knee. The meat fell back on the plate and she started laughing. My father couldn't take his eyes off her.

"Fine. Their class won. Slavka got a certificate."

"I see." She smiled. "Now he'll come inside and brag till the cows come home. He absolutely has to win."

We ate in silence for probably a minute. My father wasn't eating.

"Why are you looking at me like that?" she finally said to my father.

Her voice had changed.

"You cut your hair," he said.

"And so? Now I'm not allowed to cut my hair?"

"It's a new hairstyle."

"Listen, let's not do this in front of your son. Reporters from the States come to see us at the office, and you want me to look like a scarecrow."

"It was a pretty hairstyle."

"It aged me. Don't you understand? I looked forty. But I'm thirty-two. I'm only thirty-two!"

"What about the reporters?"

"What?" she stammered and gave him a bewildered look.

"How old are the journalists from America? Are they young?"

Marina looked at him without saying a word. Then she pushed her plate away and rose abruptly.

"I am so fed up with this obsession of yours! We can't even eat a decent meal."

She slammed the door, and we were left sitting at the table. The meat on my father's plate was untouched.

"I apologize, Kostya," Marina said later that night, coming to see me in my room. "We spoiled your supper. This happens with us. Your father is very sensitive about the difference in our ages. And nothing I say can convince him otherwise."

"That's OK," I said. "Everyone has their problems."

"But I have absolutely no idea how to help him. I have to weigh my every step to make sure I don't say or do something. He flies off the handle at the drop of a hat. You know, I'm tired of it. Can I smoke in your room?"

"Smoke away. It's your apartment."

"Listen, what's this you have?" She leaned over the desk by the window.

"A drawing."

"This is wonderful! The children were making my ears buzz today over how you were drawing here this morning. You used up all my paper."

"I'm sorry. I'll buy some for you tomorrow."

"Oh please! That's not what I mean. This came out marvelously!"

"It's the Black Sea," I said. "There's this one great guy living there."

"Have you been there?"

"No. But I can imagine it."

"You've never seen the Black Sea?"

"No."

"Then how did you draw it?"

"I can imagine it."

"I see." She nodded warily. "But whose children are these?"

"Children?" I said, and I coughed a little.

"Is the smoke bothering you?" She fanned it away and leaned toward the open window.

"No, no, it's all right. All's well."

"For some reason they have identical faces. Look, the same face. Was that on purpose? Or are they twins?"

"Twins," I said, coughing a little more.

"So many?"

"I like it when there are lots of children."

– – –

In the summer at the beach there are always lots of them. Running and shouting. Their bellies are so round. Some wear straw hats and some have no pants on. Because their parents like to watch them naked. They run and run, and then—boom!—their little bottoms land softly in the sand. But only to a certain age.

They weren't taking my pants off anymore when Mama and I hid from the sun under our umbrella and my father played volleyball. Evidently neither one was interested in me anymore. With or without pants. It didn't matter.

Because those young women were there. And my father was playing with them.

The ball sails over our heads. Smack! A ringing blow. My eyes follow its flight. I hear them laughing. Once more—smack! Again I look up. The ball is turning into the sun, and I have tears streaming from my eyes. I can't see a thing. Smack! Next to me someone screams, "Get out of the water! Come here this instant! What is that you have?" Smack! "Throw that filth out this minute! You're going to get it!" Smack! "Catch it, catch it!" Smack! "Come on, come on, one more time!" Smack! And then two times quickly—smack! smack! But the sound is a little different and very close. "Did you get that?" And in reply a child's cry. "Don't cry or you'll get it again." Smack! "Look! Look! It's going into the water." Smack! Smack! "What, you haven't had enough?" Smack! "Excellent! You did it! Now let me!" Smack! Smack! Smack! "Stop your wailing. My hand's sore from all this hitting!" Smack! "It's going into the water again! She's hitting it there on purpose!" Smack! "Got it!" My father's voice.

Not at all like the voice he uses at home.

I open my eyes, turn, and look at the water. So as not to look where my mother is looking. Because she is watching them constantly. And next to us that little guy just can't quiet down. "Let me put cream on your face." She doesn't even turn her head in my direction. "I don't want it. It's stinky."

At the water's edge a dog is running behind some kids. First one way, then the other. Like a wind-up toy. She crouches on her front paws and howls. They throw sand at her.

Behind me—smack! And then it stops.

"Kostya!" My father's voice again. "Throw the ball!"

I'm sitting watching the dog. Except my back's a little tense.

"Are you deaf or something? Hey, Konstantin!"

Behind me, soft steps across the sand. My mother raises her head higher and higher. She stops. She looks somewhere behind me and straight up. It's not my father. She looks at him differently.

Next to me on the sand is a shadow.

"I'll bring it right over." A woman's voice. "All's well. The boy just got distracted." I look at the shadow.

Long hair. Not at all like Mama's. The shadow contracted and got big again immediately. "Catch!"

Smack!

"Why don't you ever play with us? Last time you sat there like that, too. And the time before that."

My mother looks at her but doesn't answer. The sun has turned her pupils to black dots.

"Where have you run off to?" My father's voice. "Let's hurry this up!"

Smack!

The shadow sways and vanishes. My mother starts lowering her head. Her pupils shudder and start to enlarge. And around them are these bright specks.

– – –

I probably should have stood up and thrown them the ball. Then she wouldn't have come over and my father wouldn't have said later, in the car, that my mother was a jealous ninny. Or even better, I should have stabbed this ball with a knife. A nice sharp one. My father had cut his finger when he was treating everyone to watermelon. And the woman with the long hair had watched him and laughed. As if she were being tickled. The juice ran down her fingers.

"Why aren't you eating?" my father said. "Distracted again, are you?"

She was standing there and laughing. And my mother was sitting under her umbrella. Looking at the water.

I should have thrown them the ball.

Although, whether I had or not wouldn't have made anyone have a better time. My father would have kept on playing his volleyball on the beach. When fall came, we started taking outings to the forest. Each Saturday morning he started pacing around the apartment and whistling something. My mother always told him not to whistle in the house, but he sat down in the kitchen and whistled even louder. "Do you like soccer, Kostya?" I said I did. "Then get your things. We're going to the forest."

It was better in the forest than at home. You could find hawberries and spit the seeds at that girl with the long hair. From the bushes. Where no one could see you. Or snarl burdock in her hair. But I chickened out when it came to the burdock. I just imagined her cutting it out with scissors. Imagined it and spat hawberry seeds. Until they dragged me out of the bushes.

"Quit horsing around. Let's play soccer."

But I wasn't horsing around. I was trying to hit her in the head.

"You play offense. And I'll stand in the goal," my father said. "We'll play to ten."

Except that he didn't stand in the goal. He made stupid faces and started whistling again. But Mama wasn't saying anything to him anymore. She was sitting by a tree watching us. Probably it only mattered to her that he not whistle at home. I don't know. At the time I didn't understand it. I just ran toward the other goal and kicked. But we still let more by. Because he let that girl score on purpose.

"They're girls. What are you so upset about? We're not going to play them seriously."

But I was hurt. Because I'd been trying. I really wanted to beat them. And he let them score in the beginning on purpose so that the score ended up five to nine. And when there was just one goal left for them to win, he suddenly started trapping them. I thought, now we might pull it off. I started running faster and equalized. Something hurt in my stomach, but we were just one goal behind. And that girl with the long hair was running around me and laughing. But I wasn't laughing. Because I only had to kick in one goal. And I thought now we would pull it off. But my stomach hurt bad. And that was when he caught the ball and threw it right at her feet. I saw him throw it to her on purpose, but I still took off. Because I thought I'd make it. But I tripped and hit my head. And when I looked up they were hugging. And she was shouting, We won! I stood up and went into the bushes. Because I didn't want them to see me crying. And because my stomach hurt so bad.

− − −

That evening the doctor came and said it was appendicitis. He pressed slowly on my belly and then released very abruptly. I bounced up from the pain. Like that ball I'd wanted to stab.

We sat on a stretcher in the ambulance, and my father stroked my head. I told him that if I died he shouldn't take that girl with the long hair into the forest anymore. He laughed and said I was a ninny. An appendectomy was a very simple operation.

– – –

Jealousy is the kind of thing you just can't beat. Ever. No matter how hard you try. There are strong people who can beat anything—enemies, friends, loneliness. But jealousy is a whole different thing. You just have to go and cut out your heart. Because that's where it lives. Otherwise, every movement you make is going to be aimed at you. It's like drowning in quicksand. The harder you try to get out, the faster you sink into the quagmire. Pretty soon only your eyes are left on the surface. Your burning eyes. All kinds of crap have already washed into your nose. Go ahead, breathe in. Either way you've got less than a minute left. Bye-bye, wide world. It's been swell.

Until that bitch showed up.

"When I get home I'm going to kill her, damn it," one sergeant in the hospital told me after they had evacuated us from Chechnya.

"You're nuts. What for?" I said. "She doesn't even know you lost your leg."

"She'll find out. And then there's no fucking way I'll hold on to her. You know how many guys are running around there, at home, with legs? Running around all over town, the bastards, and each one of them has two damn legs poking out."

I looked at him but didn't say anything.

"If I catch the bastard who stretched that trip-wire next to the checkpoint, I'll show him what legs are for. The way they taught us in school. With feeling."

A special forces guy hung suspended in the ward next to me. He was brought in after they did my second operation. He hung there in a sling made out of sheets, because he'd been run over by the back wheel of a truck and he had no pelvis left. All his bones were broken, jumbled up in a heap. Like children's toys you're sick of so you dump them in a corner.

They sewed a rubber hose into his belly and attached a bottle to the hose. That's how he went to the toilet. I mean, he didn't actually go anywhere, he just hung there in his sling, and occasionally they changed the bottle. Emptied it and brought it back.

Twice he managed to accumulate enough pills. But doctors being doctors, they pumped out his stomach. They didn't care what his life was going to be like. True, later the head doctor gave him his word that everything would be set right so he stopped hiding pills in his pillowcase. Everything being set right was important to him.

"So what about you?" he asked me. "Do you have a girl back home?"

I said I didn't.

"That's good. Otherwise she'd leave you. Have you seen what you've got under the bandages?"

"No. There's no mirror in the bandaging room."

I was lying. There was a mirror in the bandaging room. For the nurses. In a military hospital where it's all guys lying there, girls have to keep up with those things. "L'Oreal. Paris. After all, I'm worth it." Who knows where you're going to meet your destiny? Though we weren't much to write home about. If you really tried, you might make one normal guy out of three of us.

But I didn't tell the special ops guy about the mirror. First of all, I'd been too chicken to approach it. And secondly, he would never learn the truth anyway. How much longer could he hang there like that?

"Still, you've got everything working down below there," he said. "The equipment's working."

And I said, yes, that was all fine.

"But I don't know what to tell my wife, damn it. She'll probably leave me. What do you think, was the head doctor lying to me?"

"I don't know," I said. "He's a good guy generally."

But the worst part of the hospital was the dreams. Because at first, after I woke up, I wouldn't remember what had happened to us. *Like it had been cut off.* I'd even forget climbing into the APC. I'd lie there in my bandages, moaning, unable to remember a thing. It hurt, so I'd just wait for the nurse. And her cool hands. Even through the bandages I could feel them.

At first I didn't know what they called that, but then I heard. Someone said, "Promedol." And they also said, "Why are you using so much on him? You've still got two whole wards to go." Then, her cool hands, the shot in my upper arm—right through the scab, which crackled a little—and the darkness began to rock. It waltzed and kept retreating. And her voice. "Do you know how much this hurts him? Let him get a little sleep." Her voice swayed with the darkness, turned into a white ribbon, and melted. "Do you know what he was like when they brought him in?"

That's why I was always waiting for her to come. And bring her melting voice. "I'm coming, I'm coming, don't rush. What's with you? Hold on just a little longer."

Then I started dreaming and started to dread her arrival. Because I *remembered*. I dreamed about it all.

– – –

"Damn, he's alive! He's alive!" Genka shouts. "Pull him out! He's burning up there!"

"There's a fucking horde of snipers around us!" Seryoga's voice. "I can't crawl over there again."

"Crawl! Can't you see my leg's busted? Crawl! I can't get him! Pashka! Do you hear me? Pashka? There's a sniper in the window over there. Take him out when Seryoga runs back to the APC. And I'll shoot the fuck out of the ones over there. Give me another gun!

Where is that shitass captain? Let's do this, Seryoga! All set? One, two, three! Go!"

Chaotic shooting from several submachine guns. Then a loud boom.

"Fuck you, bastards!" Genka shouts. "Pashka! Hit him with another grenade!"

Seryoga leaps toward me in the APC, shielding himself from the fire with his arms. The bullets are raining down. Crackling on the armor.

"Kostya! Kostya!" he shouts. "Are you alive? Can you hear me?"

I open my mouth. There's a look of horror on Seryoga's face. He puts the fire out on me with his bare hands. I want to close my eyes, but I don't have any eyelids. They've been burned off.

"We'll pull you out right away! The captain's gone for help. They killed the ensign, Demidov. And smashed his player to pieces. Lord, how can this be? You're burned to a crisp! I thought you were dead! Kostya, forgive me! Kostya! I thought you were dead!"

"Seryoga!" Genka's voice. "Where the hell are you? Pull him out of there and fast! We have to get away! We can't hold on here long! I'm nearly out of bullets!"

Again, a gust of machine gun fire. Then a loud grenade launcher.

"Pashka! All set? One, two, three! Come on, Seryoga! Go!"

Seryoga leans over me, and I wake up from the pain. That's how I remembered. In a dream.

That's why I was afraid to go to sleep now. I was terrified when she came with her shot.

"Hey, what's the matter? Why are you so upset? I'll give you a nice shot and you'll fall asleep in a flash. You're completely worn out. It's all right, two more minutes and it won't hurt. Hold on, it'll be over soon."

– – –

"How's that? Does your tummy hurt?" the doctor said, leaning over me. "It's nothing so terrible. Appendicitis is a very minor matter. We'll put you to sleep now, and when you wake up it'll all be fine. See, over there, at the end of the hallway? The light? Go there. That's the OR."

He and my father stayed in the room where they'd undressed me, and I headed off into the darkness. The floor was cold.

"Don't stand around barefoot!" the doctor shouted at my back. "Climb onto the table and lie there. I'll be right in."

All I'm wearing is a shirt that reaches nearly to the floor. There's a cutout on the right side. Round, like an apple, but a little bigger. As if someone had torn the shirt with a watermelon. Kind of a small watermelon. I touch my belly through the hole and keep going. It's dark all around. Only ahead of me light falls from the open door. No one's there. I'm walking—one step, another. It's hard to walk any faster. It hurts where the cutout is on my shirt. And my feet are freezing. It's dark.

But there's no one in the room. It's light, but it's still cold. Because it's autumn, and Mama keeps going on and on about how we obviously can't expect any heat from the house management. You could take them to court, those miserable idiots, and they'd still just drink their vodka and curse over the phone. Dress warmer, Kostya. Or you'll catch cold and have to miss school. Where's your sweater?

Where? Under the couch, that's where. I wore it once and the kids in the yard started teasing me and calling me "sunflower." Little yellow birds and pink flowers.

But now I wouldn't mind. I'd pull it right over this shirt with the hole and curl up in a ball somewhere. Because it hurts. I'm a little sick to my stomach, too. But there isn't anywhere to curl up. In the middle of the room there's just this ironing board. Mama has one exactly like it. But without the straps. She doesn't have a lamp like this, either. It's huge—bigger than a washbasin. And there are four more switched on inside it. A real spotlight. We don't need one like that for ironing. I always help her iron.

"What are you doing on the floor?" The doctor's voice reached me from the hall. "All right now, get up! I told you to climb onto the table. Why did you lie down on the floor?"

"It's too skinny. I'll fall off."

"Climb up! Enough chatter. Help him. He'll never get up like that."

I turned my head and saw feet in women's shoes coming toward me. The doctor kept talking somewhere behind me. A man's voice: "Great, he decided to stage a sit-in. Lift him onto the table."

Her hands were cold, too, but I didn't care anymore.

"OK, scoot up a little."

"It hurts."

"I know. Now you're going to breathe into the mask and it will all go away."

"What mask?"

"Raise up a little and I'll show you."

The table was very narrow. She looked at me with the dark half of her face and strapped in my arms.

"What's this, are you going to cry now?" The voice under her surgical mask was different now. "You're our future soldier. Soldiers don't cry. Do you like to watch war movies? What? Speak up. Why are you whispering?"

I repeated, "I like them."

"There you go. And you know how soldiers sometimes get hurt? But they don't cry. They have to be brave. Will you be brave when you go to war?"

I nodded, but I couldn't wipe away the tears. She'd strapped down both my arms.

"Good boy. Now I'm going to put some cream there. It'll be a little cold, but you be brave. All right?"

I nodded, and she put something wet there, where the hole was in my shirt.

I couldn't see what she was putting on there. It just felt sticky. And even colder.

"Let's have the anesthesia," the doctor said. He had a mask on his face, too.

"Don't be afraid, little one," she said. "Is the mask on snug? Don't turn your head."

But I wasn't. I was trying to nod that it was on snug.

"Now I'm going to turn on the gas for you, and you start counting from one hundred to one. Backwards. Understand? Don't turn your head."

I started counting. But then I got mixed up because I was trying to keep my eyes open. So they wouldn't think I'd fallen asleep. And start cutting.

"Are you counting? Now stop turning your head! Think about something nice."

But suddenly I saw that girl with the long hair. I saw her running toward the goal and scoring a point against my father. And then my eyes just closed. I was about to tell them something but couldn't. I think it was about how I should count over.

– – –

"Where's Pashka?" I said, getting into the front seat of Genka's SUV. "Have you two had another fight or something?"

"Today we're going to look for Seryoga without him," Genka replied. "He's got problems at home."

"Why didn't you come yesterday?"

"Yesterday we both had problems."

"I waited for you."

"That's OK." Genka snickered. "You've got yourself a new family now. I'll bet you found ways to fill the time."

"Yeah. I took my brother to Happy Starts at school."

"What's wrong with that mama of his? Did she dump the kid on you or something?"

"Cut it out. She had some American journalists coming to see her. She was busy with them."

"American?" He snickered again. "And where's your father looking? They'll carry that babe off. She's not half bad."

"Hey, it's all for her work."

"I know about that work of theirs. They're always fucking in those offices of theirs. I wouldn't mind getting to know that babe myself. For the purpose of mutual and disinterested love. Your father's pretty old. She must be tired of him. What do you think, could she love a veteran of the Chechen War? Or do you have the hots for her yourself? Eh, Konstantin?"

I didn't say a word and started taking off my jacket. The car heater was going full blast.

"Are you mad, Kostya? What do you care? She's nobody to you. And by the way, you didn't even want to see your own father. If it weren't for me, you wouldn't have stayed with them at all."

"I'm not mad," I said.

"Toss it over there, on the back seat. Why are you crushing it in your hands?"

I turned around to put the jacket down, at which point a piece of paper fell out of the pocket.

"Got it!" He caught it, still steering the SUV with one hand. "What's this you've got here? Did you draw this yourself? Damn if you can't draw! Not too shabby! Why didn't you ever tell me?"

"I just started drawing yesterday."

"Cut it out!" He kept one eye on the road and examined the page with the other. "You mean you learned to draw like that all at once?"

"I drew a little before the army. There was this guy who made me."

"Smart man. Tell him thank you. And you say babes don't interest you. Just look what a hot one you drew! And with long hair, too! You know how much I love long-haired babes! Who is it?"

"A friend of my father's."

"Listen, your old man is something else! He looks like a real old fart, but he's got babes swarming around him. Those young ones just glom on to the old guy. I've got to get a consultation with him."

"She must be about forty now."

"Yeah?" He took his eyes off the road to study her face more closely. "Then why does she look so young? Are you having me on? Listen, you're really strange today."

"Watch the road or we'll hit something."

"I am watching. You're the one who doesn't want to tell me about the babe."

"There's nothing to tell. I was little back then."

– – –

But now I'm big. So is Genka. We've grown up and we're driving from train station to train station, looking for Seryoga. Who's nowhere to be found. None of the homeless guys, none of the police—no one knows anything. And Genka can't stand cops. I do the talking and he looks off to the side. Or says he's going to buy some cigarettes. Eventually you get back in the car, and there's always something crunching underfoot. The SUV is full of trash. Parliaments or Davidoffs. Because Genka only buys the expensive kind. The dream of an idiot comes true. An American SUV. Cigarettes littering the floor. Not even Marlboros. In grade school he probably scavenged cigarette butts. "Hey, buddy, how about a smoke?" A conversation next to the Palace of Culture. What I'd like to know is where that Fryazino guy's been hanging out.

"Did you shake down kids when you were young?"

He gives me a look of incomprehension.

"I'm saying, did you take other kids' kopeks?"

"Oh! That's what you mean!" He smiles, recalling. "Yeah, sure. What did you expect?"

I didn't expect anything. It was obvious he hadn't gone to the conservatory.

"Did you beat them up?"

"Who?"

"The kids you were shaking down."

"Sometimes yes, sometimes no. I did like to fight, though. You're standing there, you're still talking to him, but in your mind you're already…you know…it's fun. And you get this funny feeling in your stomach. Like it's cold."

– – –

The policeman is wearing a leather jacket. Black, shiny, and very smooth. It fits him like a box and barely bends at the elbows. A medieval sentry in armor. What do they have to kill to skin a hide that thick? The crown on his cap is like a monument to Gagarin's space flight. A little laughing face that doesn't care it's little. The main thing is there's a cockade above it. And two narrow stripes. But wider than the possibility of us telling the bastard to go to hell. A lot wider. And a little pink bump under his left eye. Maybe a mole, maybe something else.

That's exactly where Genka socked him—on that bump.

I always wondered what kind of people went to work there. His parents probably came to Moscow under the quota for the Workers Red Banner Plant or some such, repairing radio receivers. About twenty years ago. Then they started writing to their relatives, We're Muscovites now! When you write, it actually feels good. That's how you begin the letter. But you don't invite them to come see your little boy. Because it's a communal apartment. And you'd have to put them up. And for more than one day. You can't say, Come visit and see the Metro we have here! We'll ride on the escalator and in the evening we'll put you on a train back. What would they say at home? What kind of Muscovites are you? Hell, it's a communal apartment all the way to Khimki practically. The quota! Let them try to make it here. But your mother writes telling you to come see the grandkids. Your brother has had three for a long time. In the fall we slaughtered a hog. You could at least take a little lard back. Vitka's still drinking, though. Is it hard to find pork there in Moscow? The return address on the envelope is the village of Zvizzhi. And at the letter's close, as always, "Byby."

All one word, and without any *e*'s. How can you answer her? You'd have to bring presents and you don't make that much money. As a result, a full twenty years pass. The plant's finally given you an apartment. Two rooms. But your mother's dead by now. And Uncle Vitya's destroyed himself with drink. So you have to think of your son. There's your brother, too, but you don't get along so well with him. He came to visit about eight years ago. He had a few drinks and picked a fight. He said, Your son's just the same. The same as what? Great guy. When the time came he went to work for the police. Such is life.

And here Genka and I walk up to him and Genka punches him in the face.

"You're fools," Marina said. "Fighting with the police."

"Don't use that stuff," said Genka. "It'll sting."

"You fought in Chechnya, and now you're afraid of antiseptic. Wait, don't turn your head. I'm just about to put some on."

"Don't use antiseptic. I'm telling you, I don't like it."

"Who does? You should see my children howling over it. What, did the police make you fight?"

But we didn't fight them. It's just that this little cop said that with my face I should be sitting at home, not driving around the stations. So I don't scare the passengers. And he took away Seryoga's photo ID. Especially since Genka didn't have his passport with him. As far as my face goes, that policeman was just joking really.

Only Genka didn't get his humor at all.

On the other hand, we did find the captain.

– – –

"Which captain is that?" Marina said when she had cleared all the medications off the table.

"Ours. The one we were riding with in the APC. After the grenade hit the armor, he ran to the checkpoint. To get our guys. His legs were OK. If it hadn't been for him, the snipers would have picked us off by the APC. We all would have been left there."

Marina froze in the middle of the kitchen, holding the teakettle, and looked at Genka. Then at me. Then back at Genka.

"What?" he said. "I'm not going to let you put on any more antiseptic."

"How could that be?" she said. "You're boys."

"Well it wasn't girls shooting at us from the roofs there, either. Although sometimes there are girls, too. Once we were doing a sweep of a block and in the attic of this school—"

I gave Genka a swift kick under the table. He stopped talking and stared at me.

"And what?" Marina said, pouring the tea. "What happened at that school?"

"Nothing," he said. "Could you put some more of that antiseptic on me? I think we missed one bruise. And while you're at it I'll tell you about the captain."

When my father walked in, she was holding Genka's head to her breast with one arm and fanning him with the other and at the same time blowing on his forehead.

"Hello," my father said. "What is this very interesting situation you have going on here?"

"Hi," I said. "Marina's fixing us up."

"Fixing you up?" His expression grew even more distant. "Where are the children?"

Marina released Genka's head.

"I'll bring them home now."

"H'lo," said Genka, rubbing his forehead.

"What's happened here?"

He dropped his briefcase on the floor.

"Don't you want to take your coat off first?" Marina said.

Her voice changed, too, all of a sudden.

"Konstantin, I'm waiting for an explanation. Konstantin, do you hear me? Kostya!" my father said.

I heard him. Just as well as I had that time in the car. Jealous ninny, he'd told her. Jealous ninny. Who needs you and your jealousy? You sit there like an old sock while everyone else is having a good time. But my mother looked at him in silence. Although she'd heard him just fine, too. Only her chin started to tremble.

"Do you hear me, Kostya?"

"I hear you. You don't have to shout."

"What? What's that you said?"

"I told you to shut up."

Marina turned sharply and grabbed my arm.

"Kostya, wait!"

"No, Marina, get away from him! What did you say to me, son?"

"I'm not your son. Your son was killed in Grozny when our APC burned up. I'm a different man. That boy who was afraid of you was left behind in that APC."

"Hold on, both of you!" Marina rushed first to him and then to me. "Nikolai! The boys just got into a fight with the police. They took away the photograph of the boy they're looking for. What's his name? I can't remember! But then that captain came to their rescue. Remember? Kostya was telling us how they were riding together in Grozny the day it all happened. He works for the police at the train station. He saw the boys there, but the policemen were already beating them. He also promised to help them find this boy. I can't remember his name!"

"Sergey," Genka said. "The boy's name is Sergey. Except that he hasn't been a boy for a long time."

"Really?" my father said. "Why didn't you tell me all this to begin with?"

"You weren't listening," I said. "Let's go, Genka."

"Won't you stay?" Marina said.

"No," I said.

– – –

Genka didn't want to take me to Podolsk. He said
I should spend the night with him. His mother-in-law
was away visiting relatives in Ryazan.

"I wish she'd park herself there for good."

"Problems?"

He didn't answer, but I could tell from his face the
answer was yes. I pictured his wife, rounded her shoulders, added more wrinkles, made her hair frizzier, put
a house robe on her, and looked at what came of that.
Then I drew Genka beside her. What he would be like in
thirty years. Then Pashka, then Marina, then myself. We
were all small and fit into the lower right-hand corner
of the page. The rest of the space was left blank. It felt
like there should be something there, but I wasn't quite
ready to confront that.

My face was the easiest of all to draw. It didn't age. It
just got darker.

"What's on your mind?" Genka said.

"Nothing. I was just thinking about what's going to
happen to us."

"What's there to think? We'll be there soon and we'll
get some vodka."

I was with him on the vodka. After all we'd been through, it would have been hard to get along without it. Possible, but not very satisfactory.

"Wait up," Genka said when everyone had gone to bed. "I'm going to try to guess who this is."

He poured a glass for us both, took a sip, and looked at my drawings.

"The deputy platoon commander. Right? They shot out his lung in Urus-Martan. I remember. OK, give me another."

I drew, and he frowned and poured some more vodka.

"I can't seem to remember this one. Who is it?"

I added the helmet with earphones.

"Ah! That's Petka, the driver from the transport brigade."

I drew some more.

"Tanechka the nurse…the gunners—I traded them alcohol for boots…the battalion commander…And this…wait a minute…What do you have here?"

"It's the explosion. The cumulative charge is burning through the armor. Or at least that's how I think it would burn through it."

"I get it. And what's this?"

"Those are the spooks firing from the roofs."

"Where are they? All you've got here is windows."

"Look at the flashes. See? Each flash is a shot."

"So you draw everything in plain pencil. Hell, what you have is all gray. Wait, I'll find a colored one from my daughter. What kind should I bring you? Or do you want them all?"

"No, don't. You'll wake her."

But he goes, kicking the table on his way. While he's gone, I keep drawing. Returning, he bumps into the table again and scatters a handful of colored pencils over the floor.

"Hey, quit it," I say. "I like the plain one better."

"Oh, man…" he says, breathing the sweet smell of vodka on my cheek.

He looks at the APC that was ambushed on the narrow street and that would be history in a minute. He looks at the soldier with the busted chest being taken out of the IFV. He looks at another soldier whose belly is being sewn up right there on the ground. He looks at the body flying up from the explosion of the antipersonnel mine. He looks at our guys running for cover, hunched over, one of them waving his arms and perching like a bird when a bullet hits him, but he still hasn't figured it out. Genka watches me draw, and I listen to his breathing behind me.

"Wait up. What's that?"

"That's our lieutenant. With his children."

"But they killed him. You've got him looking thirty-five. He was young. He didn't have any children."

"What of it?" I say. "Here he is with his children. Couldn't he have had children afterward?"

Genka is quiet for a long time. He looks at my drawings.

"You know what?" he says at last. "Give me them. All of them."

"Take them," I say. "I wasn't drawing them for any reason."

— — —

The next morning we picked up Pashka and the three of us headed for Yaroslavl. Genka said that maybe one of our brother soldiers had heard something about Seryoga. He could have gone off anywhere. One guy from our company was living in Yaroslavl.

"There's no sense making the rounds of the stations anymore. We've talked to all the homeless guys. Pashka, did you see how the cops busted our chops?"

Genka turned toward the back seat and showed Pashka his face. I looked at it, too, even though I'd seen the bruises lots of times. It's just that this was the first time in all this while that Genka had said anything to Pashka.

Pashka jerked toward the window as if he were about to turn away, but that ugly face was staring at him. Slathered with antiseptic. I don't know why Genka went on the attack.

"Do you know the kind of drawings Kostya's doing? It's crazy! I'll show you later. All our guys are there, in the drawings."

We drove around every day. We were in Tver and we were in Kaluga. We drove to Vladimir. We hit five towns in one week. I'd spend the night in Fryazino, with either Genka or Pashka, and in the morning we'd get into the SUV again and drive to see one of the guys we'd served with in Chechnya. We drank vodka, talked, reminisced about the war, listened to family stories. Sometimes I'd say I was going out to smoke, and for a long time I'd stand in some entryway, shivering from the cold and exhaling transparent steam into the dark air. The first five minutes were to calm down, and the rest to finish drawing in my head what there hadn't been enough destiny for.

For one I added a leg, for another a wife. For a third his dead friends. For a fourth, a child that was healthy. I made these guys strong, their wives beautiful, and their children cute. I drew what they didn't have. I wouldn't have been able to do that with pencil.

But not one of them knew anything about Seryoga.

"Where did you run off to again?" Genka said when I got back to the kitchen, where there was nothing to breathe because of the cigarette smoke.

"I was smoking."

"All tanked up? Let's do it, then. Another go-round today."

"It's been swell, bro," he said in parting. "Can we bring you any medicine? What did the doctors prescribe for you?"

And inconspicuously we started making a second round of all the same places. Some places a third. It depended on whether we could bring them everything at once.

"Look here, this is for your liver. This is for circulation. They told me at the pharmacy it helps. Terrific stuff. You'll be running on the ceiling. And these are vitamins. They're good, too."

"What about the blood pressure cuff?"

Genka looked at him, then me, then Pashka.

"Damn! Why didn't you remind me? All right, bro, we'll bring you a cuff next time."

Then he started leaving them money.

"You know, you take it, buy something for yourself. Or your wife. It's not much, but why the fuck should we be running back and forth? Hey, it's fine, cut that out. We'll settle up later. It's a round world—nothing's fucking falling off. What goes around comes around."

Pashka watched Genka handing out money, and it felt to me he was sitting differently in the back seat now that we were driving home. Not so that he'd sit in front, of course, because I didn't care where he sat, but not all the way in the corner anymore, up against the door, and his face ninety degrees from the spot where the back of Genka's head began.

Except we never did learn anything about Seryoga.

– – –

How do you draw waiting? A continuous straight line that never runs into anything? All that's left on the page is a memory. White and square. Though it could be a drawing. A cat or a dog. Or a child and a house. But you started by drawing a line. And now you can't stop.

A Russian woman in Grozny. About fifty. She started crying when we drove up and jumped out of the APC. Or maybe she'd been crying before we arrived. Because her husband was a Chechen. They'd studied together at the teachers college. He'd been beaten to death in a jail cell in Chernokozovo. By our guys. Before the war he'd taught biology. Later she hid in a cellar with some other Russian women and all their children. Until Chechens threw grenades in there. First one, then another, and then, she thought, a third. She doesn't remember exactly. All she knows is that she has no one left. She remembers the explosions, and she still remembers the faces of her children. "A man sits in prison and he has a sentence. He knows what to expect. I don't even have a sentence." The rain on her face is very fine, and we're standing in puddles. Our machine guns are clanking because we're stepping through puddles. We're waiting for an order. No one's even smoking.

How do you draw waiting?

The straight line breaks up into a zigzag and sketches a net of rain. Trees emerge, then a road, low clouds, and finally the three of us. We're gliding above the road like three dark shadows. There's no one up ahead. Just a crow bursting out of a tree, cawing. We dissolve in a shroud.

The piece of paper is turning gray.

— — —

"Wait for me here," says Pashka getting out of the car. "I have to buy something for home."

As soon as he slams the door, Genka lights up and starts tapping his fingers on the steering wheel.

"Cut it out," I say a minute later.

"What?"

And he has this puzzled look. As if he just woke up.

"Stop tapping."

"Oh!" He nods at me. "Right."

And another minute later:

"Listen, Kostya?"

"What?"

"About those drawings of yours…"

"Which ones?"

"Oh, you remember, you drew them at my house. About the war."

"Yeah."

He's silent for a minute and takes three quick puffs.

"They killed a lot of our guys there. I feel sorry for the lieutenant. Remember him?"

I nod, though I know he's not looking at me. I know he knows I nodded.

Because it's an idiotic question.

Or maybe not so idiotic if you think how much time the lieutenant had to make us able to remember him. Two weeks. One week plus five days. Because by the thirteenth day he was "shipment no. 200." Though he said he didn't believe in the number thirteen. Or black cats. Or any of that shit. They told him at school none of that existed. There was nothing but tactical ability and the enemy. But we knew all of it existed. And learned how to cross ourselves. In the beginning it doesn't come out right because your hand's stiff. You tap your forehead and belly—so far so good, because you know for sure you have to do the forehead and belly—but when it comes to the shoulders and which one comes first, that's a problem. In the beginning we couldn't remember whether it was the right or the left. Some never got the chance to remember. Which made us try to pay even more attention to the shoulders. Because who the hell knew? What if he tripped on that wire right after he crossed himself the wrong way?

Eventually, though, it gets easier. The hand picks up the habit. It slips around all by itself. You have only to sling your machine-gun across your shoulder. Or hear them shouting there in the ruins.

Right shoulder then left. Right then left. Not like in your copybook. The opposite. There and here, there and here. Like the bolt on a machinegun. Just not so fast. Because it's a hand, after all, not a bolt. But if you could, you'd swipe it as fast as a bolt. Because you have to.

In the ruins they're shouting, Allahu Akbar! And then you start, first right, then left. You don't mix it up anymore.

"Remember the lieutenant?" Genka says.

I nod in reply.

Forehead and belly. To make sure. Maybe two snipers fired at the same time. I don't know. There's probably some competition. They were paid more for officers. I wonder which one of them got it for our lieutenant.

First forehead, then belly, then right shoulder, then left. It's important not to mess it up. The priest who taught us all how to make the cross was telling us something on that topic. About why it's the forehead, and why then the belly, and then after that the right shoulder. There's a Holy Spirit in there somewhere. But the priest was killed fast and he never got to repeat it enough times for us to remember it. So we didn't.

"Company! Right shoulder forward!"

Probably the one who hit him in the forehead got the money. Though how could he prove it was his bullet? Cash is cash. The other one was probably no fool either. Who would turn down free money? He'd be sure to say he was the one who'd aimed at our lieutenant's forehead. Though all of them are such religious guys. Like, God sees everything anyway.

Except that he's Allah, not our God.

Still, money's money.

"Listen, Kostya," Genka says. "I wanted to talk to you about that dough."

"What dough?"

"You know, the money Pashka and I—"

"I've heard all this a hundred times."

"That's not it. I want to tell you another bit."

"What bit?"

"Another one."

But I already knew what he was going to tell me anyway. Because when Genka talks you know everything in advance. What he wants to say. Only the lieutenant didn't know that. While he was alive. That's why he was surprised when Genka decided to go back for the wounded guy. "We don't abandon our own, Lieutenant," he said. And I knew that was exactly what he would say. His face is always a dead giveaway. Even though he thinks he's very clever. And can outsmart everyone. I don't know. Maybe he can some people. But not me. That goes for the money, too. I mean, at first I couldn't figure out who had taken the cash, but eventually I did. After I'd ridden around in the SUV with them.

But the lieutenant says to him, "He's already dead, though." And Genka answers again, "We don't abandon our own, Lieutenant." And again I knew he'd say exactly that. But the spooks keep muttering over the radio. "Lieutenant, take your guys out of there. Hey, Lieutenant! Listen up! We're coming in for you. We're going to cut you to ribbons, alive. Take your guys out, Lieutenant." But Genka says, "Why don't you just have a nice chat with them here? With those nice Chechens." And he left. When he came back, the spooks were already calling the lieutenant by name over the radio. "Sasha, can you hear me, Sasha? Tell your people to call off that fucking helicopter. And get out of there. Get out right now." "You're a fool, Lieutenant," Genka said. "You might as well have given them your address, too." Two days later they killed the lieutenant. In the forehead and belly. Two bullets. Not even from a sniper's rifle. They fire a Kalashnikov from half a kilometer. And make grenade launchers out of ordinary pipes.

A city of craftsmen. When I was a child there was a fairy-tale film with this name.

Now Genka is looking at me and saying, "I was the one who took the money."

I watch Pashka approaching the SUV.

"Listen, Kostya." Genka touches my shoulder.

And then I say, "I know."

Pashka opens the door and sits in the back seat.

"Great!" he says. "They have everything except special plates for the microwave."

– – –

"Enough already! Forget about it," Genka said. "Don't pick that up. It's good luck that it broke."

"The kids are running around," I said. "They're gonna step on it."

So I started picking it up. Especially since I was already under the table and I was going to have to work up the energy to get back on my stool. Under the table. So my head wouldn't spin so badly.

"Watch out you don't cut yourself," Genka said from above. "How are you doing there?"

"Fine."

"Cut yourself?"

"Yeah."

My words are getting shorter and shorter because I have to work up the strength for long ones.

"We've already poured yours."

"I'll be right there."

There's something different about my voice. It's dragging. But for now I still recognize it as my voice.

"Damn they're tiny," I say in what I think is my voice.

"Use a rag," Pashka says in his voice.

"Don't have one," says Genka. "I threw it out. We've already poured ours. Where are you?"

"Here."

Genka has more words because I was in a hurry. Because I don't get off on sitting around and listening to them not talk. Why did I have to be the one to make an effort? My money wasn't there. Wherever Genka took it. That's why I said, If you don't want to, don't, but I'll probably have another. And from then on my words gradually got shorter and shorter. Not even gradually, actually pretty fast. At first I felt all smooth inside, and then my words got short. Because no one really needed them. You reach out and pour. Or just nod. Even when they aren't asking. You sit inside yourself, and it's like you're in a spaceship. You don't respond to their calls. "Earth, Earth, I can't hear you. Bad signal. Can you hear me? Over and out." The controls aren't worth a damn. Where did they put the brake? You sit and look out at the vacuum of space. In amazement. Because it's pretty murky through the portholes. Not even a blue murk. But you've got enough fuel to choke a horse. That feels good.

"Are you going to sit there long?" Genka's voice from mission control. "The vodka's gonna go bad."

"Just a sec."

You speak slowly because the signal isn't good. Bad signal. Space is full of crap—meteorites, stars, cloudiness. Cloudiness most of all. Nothing but interference. Crowding as far as the eye can see. Instead of everyone sitting home.

All of a sudden, though, the signal improves. It's almost good.

"Let's run through Seryoga's moves. Who did he pull out after us?"

"Mikhalich."

"We'll swing by driver Mikhalich's."

They were silent. I wipe my blood off the floor with my hand. It's useless. It's dripping anyway. After a silence, the signal is excellent again.

"And then?"

"Then the captain, I think."

"That means we'll swing by the captain's next."

I try to make contact. From directly under the table.

"What are you saying down there? Kostya, don't mumble. Come on, crawl out. My wife will clean it up later. Look, you've smeared blood all over the floor."

I try hard to tune in.

"The captain was first. Then Mikhalich."

Silence over the air.

"You're sure?"

"Yeah."

"Well, OK. Then we'll swing by the captain's right now. And then by Mikhalich's again."

"And by Seryoga's," I say.

"And by Seryoga's," they say.

"Because he isn't anywhere."

I climb out from under the table. Holding shards in my right hand.

"Damn it, I told you, you'll cut yourself. Give those here."

"I can do it."

But I'm very happy anyway. Because the three of us are together again. Not separate. I'm not in outer space anymore. I'm in Genka's kitchen. I picked up all the shards.

"What are you so pleased about?" Genka says.

"I'm smiling."

"I see."

"Pour."

– – –

We'd been driving around Moscow and other towns for nearly two weeks. I'd seen more in half a month in Genka's SUV than I probably had in three years. The outside world turned out to be completely different from what I'd thought, and watching it through a car window was pretty interesting. Especially since the glass was tinted. I wouldn't have refused to ride around before, for fear of frightening passersby with my face, but no one had ever really offered. Before the doctors took off all the bandages, it was still OK to walk down the street, but afterward it wasn't so great. Especially when you ran into people you knew. I don't even know who felt more awkward, me or them. Because you have to make an effort. And pretend you don't notice. That's why I mostly stayed home or in the apartments I was renovating. I dealt with the owners over the phone. And when they did come around, they weren't much interested in me. They scarcely tried to pretend.

The world out the car window looked slightly flattened, but I still enjoyed looking at it. Though it did keep running back and off to the right. Then it started running off to the left. And that was fine, too. Because Pashka had finally changed places with me. I don't know what he and Genka talked about that night I cut my hand in his kitchen, but evidently they did talk about something. And Pashka was now sitting in the front seat. And they were discussing their business. Or rather, Genka was discussing it. Pashka would nod occasionally. But this meant they were having a discussion. Pashka didn't know any other way to discuss.

I sat in the back and drew. Genka barely groused about having to drive slowly. And even stop sometimes. So I could finish drawing a dog. Or a cop. Or the girl the cop was ogling. Because there was so much of everything there. Out my window. Soon the entire floor of the car was heaped with paper.

"I'm telling you, draw with colored pencils," Genka kept repeating. "You can't tell what traffic light it is, red or green."

"The cars are moving," I said. "Can't you see? That means it's green."

"Or maybe they're stopping."

"You're the one who's stopping. Let's go. I've had enough waiting."

So we drove. And I drew. I liked drawing even better than looking out the window. I wanted to get the whole world down on paper. When I went home again. Because the television wasn't showing it right at all. I suddenly realized that it was all completely different. The lines, the color, even the light. Though it was definitely hard to draw light with plain pencil. Genka wasn't lying there. But I tried.

So that I could keep everything for when we found Seryoga.

But Seryoga was nowhere to be found. We drove around to all the train stations again, but no one there had seen him. When I was a child my mama used to say, "He's vanished into thin air." When she was waiting for Father in the evenings after work. And looking out the window. Back before he left us altogether. And I would echo, "Vanished," and she would laugh. But then she would go back to looking out the window. Like me now. Only she didn't have Genka or Pashka beside her.

She also used to say you have to know how to wait. Wait and believe. Then everything will work out. But I didn't know what she meant. That's why I waited for things I could understand: when the semester would end, when we'd have the money for a bicycle, when my math teacher would get sick, and then—when the director, Alexander Stepanovich, would come back from that Black Sea of his and we would start drawing again.

Once I told him what my mother had said about "waiting and believing." Because I personally knew that she was believing and waiting for nothing. But he told me I was a fool.

"You know what you can do with that cynicism of yours. Anyway until life smashes your face against a wall, you won't understand a thing about it. Maybe you won't even then. But if you want, I can tell you."

I said I did.

"Then listen. Waiting means experiencing gratitude. Simply rejoicing that you have something to wait for. You look out the window and think, 'Thank you, Lord. And thank you, everyone else. To the pigeon for flying past. To the dog for running by.' See?"

"No," I said.

"Well, you're a fool. If you're lucky, one day you will. And you won't be able to see the waiting behind your gratitude."

"You mean I should say thank you to the birds?"

"You're a fool," he said, and he poured himself some vodka.

But now I looked out the window of Genka's SUV and I understood what he was trying to tell me.

"Shut the window," Genka grumbled. "It's cold."

— — —

Two days later, Seryoga turned up all by himself. We were back sitting in Genka's kitchen, the three of us, and drinking tea, when the alarm went off on his SUV downstairs.

"Damn. I'm going to rip those kids' heads off!" Genka said, and he went over to the window.

By that time everyone was sick of vodka. Even Genka's wife said she couldn't yell at us anymore. "You'll have to come up with something new." So now she would sit with us, eat candies, and look through what I'd drawn. Her favorite was the Pekinese jumping in the snowdrift with a big crow hopping behind him and pulling him by the leash. The crow thought it was a mouse trying to run away.

"And what's this?" Genka's wife said.

"Those are children."

"But why are they sitting that way? They're sitting on their hands."

"Their parents have gone to a restaurant and left them with other children. They're waiting."

"But why aren't they playing?"

"They don't like these strange children."

"I see. And what's this?"

"The parents came back late, and the children had fallen asleep on the floor. Now they're picking them up. Because it's winter, and they have to put on warm jackets. But the parents are drunk and the children are sleeping."

"You mean you thought all this up?"

"No, I was remembering. I was just thinking about how to draw waiting."

"And what's this?"

"That's a man waiting for them to remove his cast. The nurse has gone out, and he's sitting and waiting. They're always going out."

"Listen," Genka said, gazing into the twilight. "Those aren't kids. There's some guy there. He's looking this way. Why the hell did he shove my car?"

"Who is it?" Genka's wife said.

"I can't make him out. It's too dark. I think it's some-one I know."

"Come on, let me look."

She went over to the window with Pashka trailing behind. I didn't go because I knew who was standing there. I didn't have to look out the window. Because this was just the way it should be. Exactly. He came and he shoved the car.

My waiting was over.

"Let's go downstairs," I said. "It's Seryoga. He forgot your apartment number."

– – –

Usually it takes about three days to get used to the idea that a friend has died. Not one and not two. Sometimes even three isn't enough. Each time you remember him, you tell yourself, He's dead. But it still feels like you're lying. Not in the sense that he isn't dead but in the sense that you're still not ready to say those words. You can say them, but they're empty. Unconnected to life. There's an emptiness between them and reality. You sense that gap, and you can't figure out what's there, inside it. So you repeat it as often as you can: he's dead, he's dead, he's gone. But you're lying anyway. At least until three days pass. Then it's pretty much OK.

Girls probably feel exactly the same way when they give birth. That is, people keep shouting, Push! Push! and then all of sudden she tells herself, I'm a mama.

How long does it take for her to understand that? In the sense of not just saying it. Probably three days, too. She walks around the maternity hospital saying, I'm a mama. They're about to bring my baby. She looks at the signs on the walls, the different posters, clutches her robe at the neck, and starts getting used to it. Ah, that's about me. I'm a mama. But it probably still takes three days or so for you to understand that you're a mama. Or that your friend is dead.

But Seryoga wasn't dead. He'd just gone missing for a couple of weeks and then turned up all on his own. And now we could go home. Or rather, I could. Because Genka and Pashka were staying in Fryazino.

– – –

There was a lot of snow in Podolsk. It crunched underfoot, clung to my hair, stuck to my boots. People were hopping off the commuter train, waving their arms, and running home. I liked walking along without hurrying. Offering my face up to the snow.

Because it was cold. And because I knew I didn't have to hurry anymore.

"Say *carpet*," a woman was telling her child.

The boy was turning his head, brushing away the snowflakes, laughing, and sucking a lollipop.

"Say *carpet*."

"Don't want to."

"Say *carpet*."

"No."

"I won't let you go until you say it."

The boy pulled the candy out of his mouth and rattled off like a machine gun: *"Parket, parket, parket!"*

She burst out laughing and said, "That's not right. Say *carpet* again."

I looked up. The snow was swirling around the streetlamps. Clouds of snow.

– – –

"Listen, are you back now?" Olga said when I opened the door to her. "I stopped by a few times. Your apartment was so quiet. I thought something might have happened."

"No, nothing happened. I just had to go to Moscow. And then we were held up. Please, come in."

"All right, just for a minute. I wanted to see whether you'd turned up."

Her eyes asked forgiveness. In advance.

"What, Nikita isn't sleeping again?" I said.

"We probably upset you."

"No, not at all, it's fine. Wait a minute, I'll be right there. Just shut the door."

When he saw me, the little boy ran into his bedroom immediately.

"How come you left your soldier guys on the rug?" I said, walking in behind him. "Men don't abandon their own. Here, take them."

He held out his hand and took his little guys from me.

"Thank you."

"Now go to bed. Chop chop."

He pulled off his pants and shirt and dove into bed.

"There now, that's enough wiggling," I said a minute later. "What are you giggling about there?"

One eye peeped out from under the blanket. Then the other. Dark as two plums.

"I know."

"What do you know?"

"I know I know."

"And what is it you know you know?"

"That you're not scary. You just have that face."

"Right, now off to sleep with you! Or else I'll call… I'll call your mama."

He giggled again and hid under the blanket.

"I won't leave until you fall asleep."

Five minutes later I noticed a piece of paper on the table. A pencil lay beside it. When Olga came in I was nearly finished.

"Whose face is this?" she said. "It looks familiar."

"Mine," I said, and I put down the pencil.

Nikita was breathing noisily under his blanket.

About the Author

Photo copyright Lutz Durstoff

Andrei Gelasimov, born in Irkutsk in 1965, studied foreign languages at Yakutsk State University and directing at the Moscow Theater Institute. He became an overnight literary sensation in Russia in 2001 when his story "A Tender Age," which he published on the Internet, was awarded a prize for the best debut. It went on to garner the Apollon Grigorev and the Belkin prizes as well, and his novels have been consistently met with critical and popular success in Russia and throughout Europe. His novel *The Gods of the Steppe*, forthcoming from AmazonCrossing, won the 2009 Russian National Bestseller literary award.

The seeming simplicity of Gelasimov's style can be attributed to his great gift, for which there is no counterpart in Russian literature. He could be called the

Russian Salinger. Just like Salinger's heroes, his are mainly children or young people, often at the age at which the painful metamorphosis from childhood to adulthood takes place. Gelasimov also understands how to sketch a psychological portrait of his characters with only a situation or a short, often comic dialogue.

Gelasimov's heroes are alone, almost as if they were encased in a cocoon. Gelasimov is not afraid to permit them an opportunity to be happy, but he does it without becoming banal. It is not the "System" that is at fault for our suffering. People cause other people to suffer, and people can make it right again. Gelasimov always keeps completely to the everyday, does not offer a commentary, and leaves room for multiple truths. If there is a moral, then he has hidden it in his works like contraband.

About the Translator

Photo copyright Raymond Yin

Marian Schwartz studied Russian and Russian literature at Harvard University, Middlebury Russian School, Leningrad State University, and the University of Texas at Austin. She is the recipient of two translation fellowships from the National Endowment for the Arts and a past president of the American Literary Translators Association.

Schwartz worked as an editor for Praeger Publishers for two years in the mid-1970s and has been working as a freelance translator since 1978. Her first book publication was *Vekhi,* the famous collection of philosophical essays on the Russian intelligentsia, published as *Landmarks* in 1977.

In addition to fiction, Schwartz has translated nonfiction in the areas of history, including four volumes in Yale's Annals of Communism series, biography, criticism, and fine arts, including a major biography of Liubov Popova published by Abrams. She is the principal English translator of the works of Nina Berberova and translated the *New York Times* best seller *The Last Tsar,* by Edvard Radzinsky. Her two most recent book translations are Valery Panyushkin's *12 Who Don't Agree: The Battle for Freedom in Putin's Russia* (Europa Editions) and Olga Slavnikova's novel *2017* (Overlook Press), and she has translated such Russian classics as Ivan Goncharov's *Oblomov* (Seven Stories Press, now out in paperback from Yale University Press), Mikhail Bulgakov's *White Guard* (Yale University Press), and Mikhail Lermontov's *Hero of Our Time* (Modern Library).

Schwartz is currently completing a translation of Mikhail Shishkin's novel *Maidenhair* for Open Letter Books.